Jacob Weber was one student that I've never forgotten. After a rocky start at Saunders, he became an academic whiz—a Harvard med school graduate turned star fertility specialist. It's too bad that the aptitude he's shown in scientific matters never extended to matters of the heart.

His schoolmate Ella Gardner is *full* of heart, from her work as a federal prosecutor to her loyalty to her family. But she's never been lucky in love, nor in fulfilling her greatest dream, becoming a mother. Now that she's turned to Dr. Weber's expert counsel as a last resort, I wonder if they both might receive an unexpected prescription…for one another.

Dear Reader,

Most of us look forward to October for the end-of-the-month treats, but we here at Silhouette Special Edition want you to experience those treats all month long—beginning, this time around, with the next book in our MOST LIKELY TO... series. In *The Pregnancy Project* by Victoria Pade, a woman who's used to getting what she wants, wants a baby. And the man she's earmarked to help her is her arrogant ex-classmate, now a brilliant, if brash, fertility expert.

Popular author Gina Wilkins brings back her acclaimed FAMILY FOUND series with *Adding to the Family,* in which a party girl turned single mother of twins needs help—and her handsome accountant *(accountant?),* a single father himself, is just the one to give it. In *She's Having a Baby,* bestselling author Marie Ferrarella continues her miniseries, THE CAMEO, with this story of a vivacious, single, pregnant woman and her devastatingly handsome—if reserved—next-door neighbor. Special Edition welcomes author Brenda Harlen and her poignant novel *Once and Again,* a heartwarming story of homecoming and second chances. *About the Boy* by Sharon DeVita is the story of a beautiful single mother, a widowed chief of police...and a matchmaking little boy. And Silhouette is thrilled to have *Blindsided* by talented author Leslie LaFoy in our lineup. When a woman who's inherited a hockey team decides that they need the best coach in the business, she applies to a man who thought he'd put his hockey days behind him. But he's been...blindsided!

So enjoy, be safe and come back in November for more. This is my favorite time of year (well, the beginning of it, anyway).

Regards,

Gail Chasan
Senior Editor

Please address questions and book requests to:
Silhouette Reader Service
U.S.: 3010 Walden Ave., P.O. Box 1325, Buffalo, NY 14269
Canadian: P.O. Box 609, Fort Erie, Ont. L2A 5X3

The Pregnancy Project

VICTORIA PADE

SPECIAL EDITION®

Published by Silhouette Books

America's Publisher of Contemporary Romance

Special thanks and acknowledgment are given to Victoria Pade for her contribution to the MOST LIKELY TO… series.

 SILHOUETTE BOOKS

ISBN 0-373-24711-7

THE PREGNANCY PROJECT

Copyright © 2005 by Harlequin Books S.A.

This edition published by arrangement with Harlequin Books S.A.

® and TM are trademarks of Harlequin Books S.A., used under license. Trademarks indicated with ® are registered in the United States Patent and Trademark Office, the Canadian Trade Marks Office and in other countries.

Visit Silhouette Books at www.eHarlequin.com

Printed in U.S.A.

Books by Victoria Pade

Silhouette Special Edition

Breaking Every Rule #402
Divine Decadence #473
Shades and Shadows #502
Shelter from the Storm #527
Twice Shy #558
Something Special #600
Out on a Limb #629
The Right Time #689
Over Easy #710
Amazing Gracie #752
Hello Again #778
Unmarried with Children #852
*Cowboy's Kin #923
*Baby My Baby #946
*Cowboy's Kiss #970
Mom for Hire #1057
*Cowboy's Lady #1106
*Cowboy's Love #1159
*The Cowboy's Ideal Wife #1185
*Baby Love #1249
*Cowboy's Caress #1311
*The Cowboy's Gift-Wrapped
    Bride #1365
*Cowboy's Baby #1389

*Baby Be Mine #1431
*On Pins and Needles #1443
Willow in Bloom #1490
†Her Baby Secret #1503
†Maybe My Baby #1515
†The Baby Surprise #1544
His Pretend Fiancée #1564
**Babies in the Bargain #1623
**Wedding Willies #1628
**Having the Bachelor's
    Baby #1658
The Pregnancy Project #1711

Silhouette Books

World's Most Eligible Bachelors
Wyoming Wrangler

Montana Mavericks:
    Wed in Whitehorn
The Marriage Bargain

The Coltons
From Boss to Bridegroom

*A Ranching Family
†Baby Times Three
**Northbridge Nuptials

VICTORIA PADE

is a native of Colorado, where she continues to live and work. Her passion—besides writing—is chocolate, which she indulges in frequently and in every form. She loves romance novels and romantic movies—the more lighthearted the better—but she likes a good, juicy mystery now and then, too.

Dear Jacob,

I wish you continued success in your academic career. Don't let memories of the past hold you back ever again.

All best wishes,

Your professor,
Gilbert Harrison

* * *

Ella,

It was a pleasure to hear of your graduation from law school. You were—and still are—one of my best and brightest. Keep reaching for the stars, and I hope you get everything you want in life.

Warmest regards,

Professor Gilbert Harrison
Saunders University

Chapter One

The waiting room of Dr. Jacob Weber's office was like most doctors' offices. Uncomfortable chairs, upholstered in a mauve tweed fabric lined teal-green walls. The chairs, which formed a U around a coffee table covered with outdated magazines, faced the half wall that separated them from the receptionist's desk. Inexpensive prints in silver frames hung on the walls—all of them some form of mauve-and-teal-green flowers—and a potted fern stood in one corner.

As Ella Gardner sat there she wondered if there was a handbook for decorators of medical offices that said mauve and teal green were calming colors, and that a token potted plant gave a homey touch. But even if that was the common perception, it didn't work for her. She didn't feel at home. She didn't feel calm. And no amount of office decoration could change the fact that she wasn't looking forward to the consultation she was waiting for with the man who had been touted in a recent article entitled The Best Healthcare Providers of Boston as the most innovative, cutting-edge fertility specialist the city had to offer.

But Jacob Weber was her last hope.

So she'd made the appointment. She'd nearly begged for it. She'd had herself put on a waiting list for cancellations when the receptionist had said there were no appointments available for two months. When that same receptionist had called yesterday to say there had, indeed, been a cancellation, Ella had juggled three other pressing duties at the office to be able to get there.

Jacob Weber was as widely known for his arrogance and bad bedside manner as he was for his expertise and use of the newest experimental techniques.

Not that his superior, pompous, self-important attitudes were news to Ella. They'd both attended Saunders University, and although Ella had been three years ahead of Jacob and had never actually been introduced to him, his reputation as the rich boy who considered himself better than everyone else had been widespread. As well, Ella's younger sister, Sara, had been in Jacob Weber's class, so Ella had heard enough about him not to doubt his current claim to fame as the best doctor with the worst disposition.

But she wasn't there to be friends with Jacob Weber. She was there in hopes that he could do what no one else had been able to do for her in the past three years—

conquer her infertility so she could have her heart's desire: a child of her own.

There was another woman in the waiting room, and after a glance at Ella, the other woman took a compact from her purse and checked to see if there was lipstick on her teeth. Ella only had on lip gloss but suddenly wondered if something about her appearance had prompted the woman to be concerned about her own.

She didn't want her insecurity to be broadcast, though, and since she'd come straight from court after filing papers in a case she was working on, she used her briefcase as a decoy, pulling it up onto her lap. Hoping it seemed as if she'd just remembered something in it, she opened the briefcase.

There was a mirror on the inside of the lid and she used that to take stock.

No, no lip gloss on her straight white teeth—it was all still on her pale-rose-colored, not-too-thick, not-too-thin lips.

Her hair was in place, too. At least as in place as it ever got. It was curly. *Very* curly. Shirley Temple curly. So she kept it chin length—just short enough to wear parted down the middle and in a supercurly bob when she wanted it down, just long enough to pull up into a scrunchee at her crown when it was too unruly to deal with and needed to simply be contained. Like today. But none of it had escaped, so it wasn't a stray corkscrew that had caused the other woman to worry.

Ella didn't wear much makeup—only blush, mascara and a little eyeliner to enhance her light-gray eyes—and none of that had melted away. And there were no smudges on her slightly turned-up nose. No ugly blemishes had cropped up on her pronounced cheekbones or on her small chin or forehead to mar her normally clear, peaches-and-cream skin, so she decided it hadn't been anything in that area that had alarmed her companion-in-waiting.

Maybe she'd spilled something from lunch down the front of her...

She tipped the briefcase lid forward just enough to reflect her clothes rather than her face, but there were no signs of salad dressing down the front of the white blouse that peeked from beneath her open suit front, and nothing dribbled down the lapels of the plum silk. A glance downward let her know that nothing had spilled into the lap of her slacks either, so she finally concluded that what had prompted the other woman to check for flaws hadn't originated in Ella's own appearance.

"Ella Gardner," the nurse called out from the doorway to the right of the reception counter.

Ella straightened almost guiltily from behind her briefcase. "That's me," she said as she closed her briefcase, grabbed her black leather purse and stood.

"I'm Marta, Dr. Weber's nurse," the portly, older woman introduced herself as Ella reached the doorway. "How are you today?"

Ella didn't want to admit she was tense, but her voice gave her away by cracking a bit when she said, "Fine, thanks."

If the nurse picked up on her anxiety she didn't show it. She merely said, "Since this is only your initial consultation I'll have you go into Dr. Weber's office. He'll be with you as soon as possible."

"Okay," Ella agreed.

She followed the older woman past an area stacked floor-to-ceiling with files, then through another section where a countertop held medical equipment and supplies. Beyond that was a hallway, lined with exam rooms on both sides, all with file cubbies attached to the walls beside them. Marta took her to the very end of the corridor, where she motioned to the office visible through the already-open door there and stepped aside for Ella to enter without her.

"Go ahead and have a seat," Marta advised, closing the door and leaving Ella alone in the room.

The inner sanctum of the beast himself.

Two women Ella worked with had had experiences with Dr. Jacob Weber—one of the paralegals and one of the research assistants.

The paralegal had actually recommended Jacob Weber to Ella even before the "Best of" article. The paralegal had heard through the grapevine that Ella was having trouble conceiving and had suggested she consider seeing the renowned infertility specialist, warning her, though, not to expect Mr. Personality. She'd said it had been worth it to her and her husband to overlook his crankiness because his treatments had resulted in a pregnancy after six years under the care of other doctors. She'd told her that Jacob Weber could definitely be a bear, though.

The research assistant, on the other hand, had said that after two visits with Weber, she and her husband had agreed they'd rather be childless than put up with him.

Now, standing in his office, waiting to see him, Ella could feel her heart beating rapidly, and she tried to slow it down by breathing deeply, steadily. She reminded herself that the paralegal was now pregnant and had returned to her regular doctor and that regardless of the poor social and personal skills of Jacob Weber, she would now have a baby. That seemed worth everything to Ella.

She set her purse on the floor beside one of two nondescript visitor's chairs facing the big oak desk and opened her briefcase a second time. Not to use the mirror again, but to take out the file folder that contained copies of all her records from her last two gynecologists. Then she closed the briefcase, put it on the floor with her purse and placed the file on the edge of the desk just in front of the visitor's chair.

But she was still too uneasy to sit, so she took a tour of the office instead, beginning with the bookshelves to the right of the desk.

Medical texts were all she found before she moved on, venturing behind the brown leather desk chair to the large window on that wall.

The window overlooked a lush green park shaded by tall elm trees. If this were her office, Ella thought, she would have placed the desk to take advantage of the view, and she wondered if Jacob Weber ever swiveled his chair around to do that. Somehow she doubted it.

Next she went to the left of the desk, stopping before the wall there that displayed framed diplomas outlining the educational history of the man she hoped could help her.

There was the diploma from Saunders University, identical to Ella's own and a second one from Harvard Medical School, as well as a certificate that proclaimed he had satisfactorily performed a residency in gynecology and obstetrics, and another certificate of completion for his fellowship in reproductive endocrinology. Surrounding the diplomas and certificates were several awards given by the American Medical Association and various other professional organizations to Dr. Jacob C. Weber.

Apparently, he lived up to his reputation as an expert in his field.

Ella just hoped he didn't live up to his other reputation.

Turning away from the display of the doctor's accomplishments, she took stock of the sofa that lined the wall behind the visitors' chairs, curious about why it and the coffee table in front of it were there at all. She could understand other medical specialties bringing entire families into the doctor's office and requiring more seating, but infertility hardly seemed to call for that.

Although, by all accounts Jacob Weber was dedicated to his work, so maybe he sometimes slept in his office, Ella thought. She knew from the "Best of" article that he wasn't married, but what about a girlfriend? she wondered, spinning on her heels again to survey the room in general in search of something that might give an indication of his personal life.

She didn't spot anything, though. No family photographs or sports trophies or even a pencil holder shaped like a golf tee to prove he had a hobby. In fact, there wasn't a single thing in the room that said anything about the man except that he was well educated, well trained and recognized for his work.

"But all work and no play—"

The door opened unceremoniously just then, and she cut her comment short, startled by the abruptness with which the man burst into the room.

It was as if a bulldozer had just barged through the wall, and she couldn't help feeling as though she'd been caught doing something she shouldn't do.

That sense was reinforced when the man raised a dark eyebrow at her and said facetiously, "Everything to your liking?"

Maybe everything except him, Ella thought. Rather than respond to his less-than-friendly greeting, she held out her hand to him. "I'm Ella Gardner," she said, hoping against hope that her name didn't ring a bell with him, that he didn't recognize it or remember it or her or the awful mess she'd been involved in at Saunders when they were both there.

Nothing seemed to strike him, though. And he either didn't see her extended hand because he was too busy glancing at the open file he'd brought in with him or he used that as an excuse not to take it. One way or another, Ella was left standing there twisting in the wind as he moved around behind his desk. And feeling all the more uncomfortable.

"Where's your husband? The consultation should include him and his work-ups, too. I won't do this twice."

"I don't have a husband. I'm divorced."

"Have a seat," he commanded without showing any reaction to the news that she was single.

He himself didn't sit, however. He remained standing as he continued to look at the papers in the file as if they were more interesting than she was.

Ella was beginning to see why people wouldn't stick with him if he wasn't someone's last resort. But he *was* her last resort, so she did as she was told, finally settling into one of the visitor's chairs.

Even once she was sitting, Jacob Weber went on with whatever it was that had his attention, as if she weren't there at all.

It gave her the opportunity to get a good look at him. He was a big man—at least an inch or two over six feet—with long legs and broad shoulders that ably carried off wearing the long white lab coat he wore over khaki slacks, a blue plaid sport shirt and a darker blue tie. Beneath the lab coat was a body that showed no signs of fat or flab, and instead appeared taut and surprisingly muscular for someone who gave every impression of being a workaholic in the extreme.

Venturing her first real glance at his face, Ella was taken aback to find him so handsome. The only picture of him that had accompanied the "Best of" article had been a profile shot taken from a distance while he'd stood at the nurse's station of a hospital. The caption had said something about it being the only photograph the fractious Dr. Jacob Weber would cooperate for, and in it he'd been nearly unrecognizable. And nowhere in any of the complaints Ella had heard about him had anyone—including her sister—mentioned that the man was drop-dead gorgeous. She could only conclude that his personality was so rotten it diminished the impact of looks that could stop traffic.

He had the facial structure of a male model—a strong chin and rugged, angular jaw with pronounced cheekbones and slightly hollowed cheeks. His bottom lip was fuller than his top but still neither could have been more perfectly shaped below a nose that was just long enough and just straight enough.

He also had great hair—a light chestnut-brown color—that he wore short all over but not too short, giving it an artfully disarrayed look. And when he finally closed the file he'd been engaged in and raised his eyes to Ella, they were so dark a blue they were almost purple and they seemed to pin her to her chair.

"Files."

It took Ella a moment to realize he was asking for—well, demanding, actually—to see *her* files now that he'd set aside the one he'd come in with. That moment of delay was enough to aggravate him because before she'd grasped what he wanted and was able to comply, he said, "You *did* bring your files, didn't you? I'm sure Bev told you to."

Bev was the receptionist, and she'd made it very clear that Dr. Weber would not consider taking her case without a full and complete history before him.

"Yes, she told me. It's here," Ella said belatedly, reaching for her own file on the edge of the desk and passing it to him as he finally sat down across from her.

Those remarkable blue eyes went back to reading

then, as if her medical information was more relevant than she was, and Ella worked to rein in her shock over his good looks and regain some control of her wits. Clearly this was a man she had to be on her toes with.

After a few minutes scanning the file—and still with his gaze trained on the pages and not on her—Jacob Weber said, "You're thirty-five."

"I am."

"In good general health."

"Yes."

"On any medication?"

"No."

"What do you do for a living?"

"I'm a federal prosecutor."

Ordinarily that prompted a response of some kind, but not from Jacob Weber. He merely took the information without comment and continued.

"After a year of not achieving pregnancy through regular, unprotected intercourse the full gamut of tests were performed and no obstacle to conception was discovered. You had eleven courses of varying drug therapies to stimulate ovulation and—again—no pregnancy," he said, interpreting what was documented in her file, all without looking at her.

"Right," she confirmed.

"I see that you did have a husband in the picture for that—your physician's notes indicate that there was normal sperm count and motility in the male. And now you've had five months of in vitro—even without a husband?"

"Yes."

"All unsuccessful?"

"Right."

He finally looked up from her file, once again leveling those amazing blue eyes on her as he set the folder on his desk and sat back in his chair. "And you expect me to do what? Perform a miracle?"

"If you have one of those hidden in your pocket, sure, I'll take it," Ella said, trying a little levity.

He didn't so much as crack a smile to be polite. He merely stared at her.

Ella wasn't sure if he actually expected another answer to his sarcastic question but since she didn't know what else to do in response to his continuing silence, she said, "I don't *expect* anything. I've heard that your success rate is better than average, even for people who have failed with every other doctor. I've also heard that you sometimes use unconventional methods that can do the trick when nothing else has. That's why I'm here. I'm willing to do whatever it takes to have a child."

"It looks to me like you already have done everything it takes. And it hasn't mattered."

"Which is why I was hoping you had something new or innovative or experimental you might try. That's also why my regular gynecologist suggested I consult you. Between the cost and the fact that I've already failed to conceive after five in vitro attempts, we agreed that it was time to go in a different direction."

"How about the direction in which you open your eyes to the fact that not everyone is meant to have kids. That some people should—and have to—just accept that they can't and get a life."

Ella wasn't unaccustomed to having to take what an abrasive judge dished out, and she called upon the controls she used in court to hold her temper now, too. "I have a life," she informed him in an even tone. "I have a home of my own, a career, a sister and brother-in-law and niece I'm very close to, friends… That isn't the point. The point is, I want a child of my own."

"To fill the gap because your marriage didn't work out?"

It took a little more will to contain herself. "I wanted a child of my own when I was married—as you've seen in my records I was married when I first started to try to get pregnant and I didn't need any gaps filled. Not then and not now. I want kids. I want a family. Most people do. It isn't a phenomenon."

"And you want it so much you'll even do it without a man?"

"I'm a very capable, independent person. Sure, it would have been nice to have the whole package, but that isn't how it worked out. The fact that it didn't doesn't change what I want, but the clock is obviously ticking for me. I don't have time to wait for Mr. Right, the sequel, to come on the scene, court me, marry me and then start all over again. And since I don't doubt that I can raise and support a child on my own, I really don't need a man."

"Apparently you need me," he said snidely.

"Oh, you better be a miracle worker," Ella muttered, deciding on the spot that either he was going to accept her as a patient or he wasn't, but that if he thought she was going to beg, he was mistaken.

After dishing out a little of his own medicine, neither of them said anything for what seemed like an eternity. His almost-purple gaze didn't waver from his scrutiny of her. She refused to squirm beneath it—if that was what he thought he could make her do.

And then, *finally,* he said, "I'm about to begin a new, short-term research project. A few select patients will undergo acupuncture performed by a Chinese practitioner of an ancient discipline called Qigong. She'll also be giving herbs that she mixes herself, and teaching meditation and relaxation techniques. There will be sessions of therapeutic massage, as well. It's a test to see if this particular form of medicine can reset the body's natural balance in order to increase the success rate for in vitro fertilization."

A tiny speck of hope sprang up in Ella. "I don't object to having in vitro again afterward," she assured in case he was thinking she wasn't a candidate because she'd already done it so often and spent so much money on it that she was now looking to do something completely different.

"There are two problems," he continued, ignoring what she'd said and making her hope waver. "I already have as many patients, *married* patients, as I need in the study, and—"

"Couldn't you make room for just one more?"

"—the other patients have already been through my orientation to explain the process and procedures." He finished his second point as if she hadn't interrupted him.

"I'd be willing to go through it all without the orientation," Ella said, hating how she'd been reduced to grasping at straws but still hoping that he wouldn't be telling her any of this unless he was actually going to include her.

"I don't practice in half measures," he informed her.

He got points for being conscientious if not for being tactful. But still Ella didn't know if he was rejecting or reluctantly accepting her.

Another silence dragged on, again with his intense eyes on her the whole while, making her worry more as each minute passed that he was going to turn her down.

"I want you to understand," he said when he deemed to speak once more. "If I allow you into the group and this doesn't work for you, I won't treat you further. In other words, I will accept you as a patient only for this study and the in vitro procedures that will follow it. If you don't conceive after a reasonable number of attempts, you have to agree that we will go our separate ways. Because, after looking at your history, I don't see where there's anything I can do for you that hasn't already been done—repeatedly. For me to go beyond this particular study would be a waste of my time and your money."

"Okay," Ella said much too quickly, jumping at the chance he seemed to be giving her.

"Before you get on the bandwagon you should also know that because I have a full caseload and so does Dr. Schwartz—"

"Dr. Schwartz is the *Chinese* doctor?" Ella asked, feeling a bit giddy with the thought that Jacob Weber wasn't turning her away cold.

"She's married to a colleague of mine, Mark Schwartz, and she took his name."

Ella couldn't suppress a smile.

"As I was saying," he continued, still without the slightest alteration in his somber demeanor. "Because of my caseload and Dr. Schwartz's schedule, all procedures will be done in the evenings, here, after office hours."

"That's fine," she assured hurriedly.

"Even with your *full* life?"

Oh, he was nasty! But Ella wasn't going to let him get the best of her. "I told you I'm willing to do whatever is necessary," she informed him.

"Well, it will be *necessary* for you to meet with me so I can outline what the study entails. And that will have to be after hours, too, because I don't have any other time for it."

He leaned forward and scanned a desk calendar. "Today is Thursday and I'm busy tonight, so that's out. I have to be at a conference all day and evening Saturday and Sunday, and Monday evening is when the study is slated to begin," he said, more as if he was thinking out loud than explaining his time constraints to her. "I can skip the conference's opening ceremony and dinner tomorrow night, but I have a meeting after that that I'll have to get to. So that has to be it. And since the hour I'm with you will be my single chance to eat, we'll have to do it over a meal."

Hardly a gracious invitation but she would take what she could get. "Just tell me where and when," she said.

He did, without missing a beat or even inquiring if

she minded going to the heart of Boston to the hotel where his conference was being held to make it convenient for him.

"I'll be there," she said after writing the time and location in her day planner and returning it to her purse.

"I'll keep your file," he informed her then, standing and taking it with him as he did. "Have Bev give you the paperwork you'll need to fill out—everyone else has already done that."

"Okay. And I'll see you tomorrow night."

His only answer was to raise an eyebrow at her just before he rounded the desk and walked out of the office as abruptly as he'd entered it, not so much as saying goodbye to her.

But despite his bad manners Ella felt relief on two fronts.

The renowned Dr. Jacob Weber was going to give her one last chance to have a baby.

And he didn't seem to remember either her name or the scandal she'd been involved in in college.

Chapter Two

Jacob Weber was awakened the next morning by warm, sloppy kisses.

"Ah, can't you wait for the alarm just one morning?" he groused, keeping his eyes closed.

His only answer was more kisses. More kisses with even more enthusiasm. On his cheek, his nose, his ear, his brow…

"Okay, okay, I get the message," he said, opening his eyes to the tiny black schnauzer puppy he'd been sharing his bed with for the past four weeks.

He couldn't be angry, though. Not when he was looking into the furry face of the three-pound dog standing on his pillow with her head down, her shiny black nose an inch away from his, her butt up and her stubby tail wagging gaily in the air.

If he didn't know better, he'd have thought she was smiling at him.

He pretended to be more peeved than he actually was now that he was awake and said, "Have you forgotten that I'm the guy who found you abandoned on the street and kept you alive by feeding you with an eyedropper and then a baby bottle until you figured out how to lap up that special formula the vet charges me an arm and leg for? The least you could do is let me sleep until six-thirty."

The schnauzer clearly had no sense of guilt. She merely barked a tiny, high-pitched yip to emphasize her point.

And her point, Jacob knew, was that she wanted to go outside. Not something he could deny her when, even though she still needed concentrated care, he was making headway in housebreaking her. But only tentative headway. Delays were not tolerated for long. Which the second yip warned him of.

"Yeah, yeah, yeah, I'm getting up," he said, rolling out of bed and reaching for the sweatpants he'd learned in the past four weeks to keep at the ready.

As he pulled them on he couldn't help chuckling at the sight of the puppy playing tug-of-war with the edge of his sheet, growling and shaking her head furiously in the battle.

"That's it, Champ, give it hell. Live up to your name. You're nothing if not feisty," he said.

The mention of feistiness brought with it another thought, this one of the woman he'd met in his office the day before. The woman who had been coming much—*much*—too easily to mind since he'd met her. Ella Gardner.

Ella Gardner.

Feisty and determined. Like Champ.

Jacob couldn't help smiling to himself when he recalled her I-don't-need-a-man speech. What had she said about herself? That she was a capable, independent person who didn't have time to wait for Mr. Right, the sequel....

"Mr. Right, the sequel," he repeated out loud, chuckling again. "I liked that one," he informed Champ as he scooped her up in one hand and took her downstairs and out the back door of his two story townhouse.

The tiny dog couldn't make it up or down the three steps that dropped to the patch of lawn he was allotted, so he deposited Champ at the bottom of them and then sat on the top one, his mind continuing to wander back a day.

To Ella Gardner.

He wasn't sure why she was sticking with him. She was pretty enough—beautiful actually. Glisteningly-bright, riotously curly blond hair. Big, sparkling silver-gray eyes with long, thick lashes. Skin like alabaster. A small, thin, pert nose. Lips that—even when she'd been telling him off—had only left him wondering if they felt as soft as they looked.

Of course that in itself—noting details of her face, wondering things like how soft her lips were—was an oddity. He'd treated beautiful women in the past. But after initially registering the woman's appearance on some level, it became something he didn't pay any more attention to than he paid to the appearance of his less-than-beautiful patients. They were all patients—

ninety-nine and nine-tenths percent *married* patients. They were his cases. His work. Certainly they weren't anything personal to him. He couldn't do his job if they were. Not legally, ethically, morally or emotionally.

Yet this one was lingering in his head the way no one before her ever had.

Was it the feistiness? he asked himself as he watched Champ wrestle fearlessly with a rubber duck that was as big as she was, and again connected the pup's dauntless spirit to Ella Gardner.

Maybe.

He liked a little spunk, he had to admit it. And Ella Gardner seemed to have that—even if she had obviously been keeping her temper in check.

But again, he had patients whose spirit he admired and not one of them had come home from the office in his head the way Ella Gardner had. Not one had been waiting for him behind his lids when he'd closed his eyes the night before. And here he was now, barely awake and thinking about her again. Her, not any of his other tenacious, strong-willed patients.

He just couldn't figure it out. He knew people who attributed attraction to some kind of questionable science and called it chemistry. That theory just hadn't ever held water for him. If it was science, it was the flimsiest kind. That's what he'd argued even with an old medical school classmate who was doing top-dollar research on pheromones for a perfume company.

But for the first time he had to concede that maybe—even if it was flimsy—chemistry between two people did exist. Because he was just stumped when it came to finding any other explanation for why the image of Ella Gardner kept following him around.

For why he kept mentally replaying their brief, all-business meeting. Every minute of it, every nuance, every expression on her face and intonation of her voice.

He just couldn't find any other explanation for why he continued to recall her sweet, clean scent greeting him when he'd walked into his office. And how much he'd liked it.

He certainly couldn't find any explanation other than chemistry for the regret he'd been suffering over not having taken the hand she'd extended to him to shake, over missing an opportunity to touch her.

And what was it—if not chemistry—that had made him ignore that simple gesture from her in the first place? he asked himself. He would have shaken any other patient's hand. But when it came to Ella Gardner there had been something about her from the instant he'd set eyes on her that had knocked him off-kilter and his instinctive response to that had been to keep his distance, to be even more formal, more remote and removed than usual.

He didn't understand it. He hadn't understood it when it had happened. And true to form, he'd retreated into that attitude that had gotten him through the earlier part of his life. That bad attitude from which he'd recently faced some old repercussions.

But a doctor just couldn't have…

What exactly was it that he had for Ella Gardner? he asked himself. Stirrings? Attraction? Some kind of unaccountable infatuation?

He didn't know what it was or what to call it.

But whatever it was that he'd had, a doctor just couldn't have it for a patient.

And she *was* a patient.

Okay, yes, it could be argued that for now she wasn't *his* patient. That during the course of treatment she would be Kim Schwartz's patient, that he wouldn't so much as examine her until after the alternative course was finished and he began the in vitro procedures. It could be argued that only *then* would Ella Gardner be *his* patient.

But he was splitting hairs and he knew it. Basically she *was* still a patient—or at least a patient-in-waiting. And he didn't get personally involved with patients or with patients-in-waiting.

Hell, he didn't get personally involved with anyone.

And that was how he liked it. How he liked his life. No personal involvements meant no complications. It meant no encumbrances. No expectations. No disappointments. Uninvolved and unattached—that was how he made sure to keep himself, focusing on his work and solely on his work. That was the way it had always been, and that was the way he wanted it to stay. The way he intended to make sure it stayed. Which was why he never let any woman get too close or stick around too long.

"So vacate the premises of my brain, Ella Gardner," he muttered under his breath, through clenched teeth.

The sound of his voice was enough to distract Champ from the rubber duck, and she did her springy little run over to him and promptly began a tug-of-war with his big toe. Which she could barely open her mouth wide enough to accommodate.

Her pin-sharp teeth hurt some, but still her struggle made Jacob laugh. He leaned forward and picked up the pup again to take her inside.

"Patients and puppies—sometimes you're both pains in my neck," he told Champ.

But he still held the tiny dog to his face, rubbing his nose in the downy fur behind one of her ears.

And in spite of all his determination to put Ella Gardner firmly out of his mind, he also still found himself—entirely against his will—looking forward to having dinner with her tonight more than he should have.

And way, way more than he wanted to.

Chapter Three

"This is Jacob Weber. I've had a patient emergency this afternoon and am running behind schedule. You'll have to meet me at my office rather than at the hotel and wait for me to finish with my other appointments today. We may or may not be eating, depending on the time left before my meeting, but I'll make sure to run you through the orientation, even if it's on the fly. Unless, of course, you aren't here when I finish for the day, and then I'll assume you've had second thoughts about this course."

Ella played the message a second time, shaking her head as she listened again. She was amazed by the doctor's curt, verging-on-rude demeanor even on the telephone. Although she supposed she should give him points for making the phone call himself, for not merely having his receptionist do it.

On the other hand, as Ella played the message a third time, she thought that he might be better off having his receptionist relay his messages. At least Bev was nice.

But Ella reminded herself that Jacob Weber was the best there was when it came to infertility, so she would just have to overlook his rotten social skills to be treated by him.

It was a shame, though, she couldn't help thinking. Because as the deep, rich tones of his voice wafted over the line for the fourth run-through of the message, the image of him spontaneously presented itself to her mind's eye—the way it had about a million times since she'd met him. It was a shame that someone with the face of a Greek god, someone with broad shoulders and smoldering nearly purple eyes, someone who exuded a raw, steamy sexuality that he didn't even seem aware of, had a gargoyle's personality. Without that he would have been a powerhouse of a man, whom no woman could resist.

Then again, maybe for her own sake it was good that he was so unlikable. Because if she was playing his phone message four times just to hear his voice and thinking yet again how great looking and sexy he was, she'd better have something that tempered what otherwise might seem like an attraction to him.

But of course she *wasn't* attracted to him. Continuing to think about how jaw-droppingly handsome he was was just like recalling an awesome winter sunset—it might be something to behold but only from the warm safety of a house where fierce winds blowing outside couldn't get in.

No, there was no way she was attracted to Jacob Weber. She needed his professional services, his talents, skills and experience as a doctor and that was all. Being attracted to him amidst that—coupled with his contrary, irritable, arrogant temperament—would be very, very bad. It was the absolute last thing she needed. Or wanted.

Still, she played the message a fifth time, telling herself it was for its supercilious, overbearing tone, and the turnoff that provided. That it was not for the sound of the polished-mahogany voice that delivered it.

Then she made herself hang up the phone.

A woman would have to be crazy or masochistic to put up with a man like that in any kind of personal relationship, she asserted to herself. And she wasn't crazy. Or masochistic. Or looking for a new relationship with any man, let alone one like Jacob Weber.

A single marriage that had demanded too long a period of suppressing her own needs and desires, a marriage in which she'd allowed herself to be controlled, was enough for her. She certainly didn't need to top it off with someone like the unpleasant doctor.

"No, thanks," she said out loud as she went into her bedroom to change out of her business suit.

"Just do your job and do it well, and I'll be only too happy never to have to see you again." She went on talking to the unseen Jacob Weber as she put on a pair of gray slacks and a white camp shirt for her second encounter with the prickly physician.

And hopefully it wouldn't take too long to accomplish the feat of getting her pregnant, she added silently, fighting against the ever-present fear that it wouldn't happen at all. Because the less time she had to spend with the man and tolerate his pomposity, the better.

"I'll be glad when you're nothing but a bad memory," she proclaimed as she scrunched the curly explosion of her hair above the rubber band that held it at her crown and retraced her steps out of her bedroom and then out of her apartment.

And that's all he'd be, too, she assured herself as she left the building and got into her car to drive to Jacob Weber's office. "Nothing but a bad, bad memory," she repeated forcefully.

Yet somewhere buried deep beneath that bravado lurked a tiny shadow of doubt.

A tiny shadow of doubt born of the fact that every time she thought about seeing the gargoyle in a Greek god's body again she felt a twinge of excitement....

"He's right behind me, I promise," Marta said to Ella as the nurse came through the door from the inner office into the waiting room where Ella had been sitting for over an hour.

"Okay," Ella answered, hoping the woman was right but unsure whether to believe it or not since Bev, the receptionist, had told her the doctor would be out after the last patient had left forty minutes ago and then repeated it when she'd left herself twenty minutes earlier.

Marta gave her a reassuring smile, said good-night, and went out.

The longer Ella sat there, the more difficult it was to avoid what she considered her pregnancy demons. The thoughts—the doubts—that crept into her mind when she wasn't guarding against them or when she had too much time on her hands.

What if nothing worked and she never got pregnant? What if all the money, all the effort, all the pain came to naught? What if she spent her entire life childless?

The questions tortured her and, as if she'd outrun them, she stood and forced herself to focus only on the present. On the fact that Jacob Weber was keeping her waiting.

Clearly the office ran on his timetable, and he wouldn't be rushed. For anyone. Certainly not for her.

Ella decided to take a stroll around the waiting room, pausing to look more closely at the framed prints on the walls, to straighten the magazines on the coffee table, to pluck a dead leaf from the fern and bury it in the soil around its roots. And all the while she wondered if Jacob Weber was making her cool her heels on purpose. Just to be contrary. Or as some kind of test.

Then, through the cut-out that connected the receptionist's area with the waiting room she saw the light in the hallway that ran between the examining rooms turn off, and she felt encouraged.

At least she did until she caught sight of the man himself opening the door to what looked like a supply closet.

Without any acknowledgment of her, or any apparent awareness that she was even out there, he slipped inside the closet and closed the door behind him.

He probably put counting cotton balls ahead of meeting with her, she thought, feeling a little surly after all the time she'd been waiting.

He was only in the supply closet for a moment, though, before he emerged again. Yet he still offered her not even a glance or a word to let her know he really was on his way before he stopped at the area where the scale and other machinery were located—the area that was apparently the nurse's work station.

Did he even know she was watching him? Ella wondered.

He didn't seem to. Or care, if he did, because for what felt like an eternity his attention was on something.

The man really was a jerk, Ella thought, staring openly at him in hopes of at least drawing a glance.

It didn't work. He went right on looking over some sort of paperwork, oblivious to her.

Jerk, jerk, jerk...

Good-looking jerk, though, she had to concede as she took in the sight of him in tan slacks and a tan sports coat over a darker brown dress shirt and tan tie that all seemed to set off his chestnut hair to perfect effect.

But again she reminded herself that he was a gargoyle in a Greek god's body so as not to let that handsome appearance cloud the reality.

After another few minutes he seemed to finish what he was doing, because he tucked the paperwork into a file and brought it to the receptionist's desk, finally gazing in Ella's direction.

But that was as much as she got.

They were only a few feet apart, and he still didn't bother to speak. He merely raised a cursory glance at her before lowering his eyes to the desk again to write something on a note he attached to the file.

Maybe he was just singularly dedicated, Ella told herself. But that didn't keep his actions from seeming just plain rude.

He finally flipped off the rest of the lights in that portion of the office and—at last—headed for the door that would bring him into the waiting room.

You'd better be damn good at what you do, Ella thought as he joined her.

She had to look twice to believe what else she was seeing, however. Riding along in the side pocket of his sports coat was what appeared to be a tiny black puppy with two front paws and a soft furry head—no bigger than a plum—sticking out of the top.

The almost-too-small-to-be-real dog barked a squeaky-but-fearless bark at her that Jacob Weber ignored as, without greeting her, he said, "I'm going to have to make a stop at my place—luckily it's just across the street. Then it looks like all we'll have time for is a fast-food dinner before I need to make my meeting. There's a hole-in-the-wall a few doors down that has Chicago-style hot dogs. We'll probably have to stand and eat them at one of the counters along the wall, but that's as good as it's going to get."

And all that without any reference whatsoever to the puppy in his pocket.

"Uh...okay," Ella said. But she refused to be left in the dark about the dog and pointed to the side of the doctor's coat. "Aren't you going to introduce us?"

Jacob Weber looked down at the coal-black face

peering with pint-size grandeur from his pocket and said, "This is Champ. Who is the cause of my need to stop at home, since I can't take her to my meeting."

"Champ is a girl?" Ella said, unable to suppress a smile at the tiny, wavy-haired terrier, or to hold out a finger to pet her.

"She is a female, yes," Jacob Weber confirmed.

"Champ makes her sound like a boy."

"She's named Champ because that's what she is—a little champ." That was all the explanation he was offering because then he said, "Shall we go? We don't have much time."

Champ was more easily won over than her owner, because she was licking Ella's hand and wiggling around in the coat pocket enough to let Ella know she was wagging her tail.

But Ella had no choice except to comply with the doctor's insistent suggestion, retrieve her hand and follow him to the door.

He opened it, waited for her to step out into the hallway and then closed and locked the door behind them.

The elevator was directly across from his office, and the moment he pushed the down button the doors opened.

"Champ looks too young to be away from her mom," Ella observed during the elevator ride that Jacob Weber would likely have left silent.

"She is. I found her in the gutter at the curb in front of my place about four weeks ago. Since she seems to be a purebred, the best guess is that her original owner was moving the litter for some reason and she somehow fell or got out of the box unnoticed. I knocked on a few doors but no one knew anything about her so I took her to a vet around the corner. He thought she was five or six days old at the time and said she wouldn't live without special care."

"And you decided to keep her and give that special care?" Ella asked, trying to keep the surprise out of her voice.

They'd reached the ground floor, and the doctor held open the door long enough for her to precede him out of the elevator.

"The vet was too busy to do it so I did," he said matter-of-factly.

"What kind of special care did she need?" Ella persisted as they left the office building.

He continued in that same no-big-deal tone to outline a regimen of feeding and watering the pup every hour round the clock until recently, of caring for her day and night to pull her through, of her still needing to be looked after closely and not left unattended for long periods.

By the time they'd walked across the street to a row of brown brick town houses, Ella was amazed that the gruff Jacob Weber had gone to such lengths to save the animal.

"You're a dog lover," she guessed.

He shrugged as he unlocked and opened his town house door, reaching in to flip on a light, then motioning her inside. "I've never had a pet of any kind before this," he said as he came in after her and closed the door behind them.

"And you still kept Champ and did all that for her?" Ella marveled.

"What was I going to do? Put her back in the gutter to die?"

That snide statement was more like what Ella expected from Jacob Weber. As was the curt "I'll only be a minute" that came next.

But for the first time she didn't take him or his surliness as seriously as she had before. How could she when, as he turned to go into what appeared to be the living room, he reached into his pocket and extracted the tiny dog to hold up to his face and say in a tender voice, "Okay little girl, outside to do your business and then I'll have to put you in the crate for a while. Don't worry, I promise it won't be long."

Then he lowered the puppy to hold to his chest just as they both disappeared from her view.

Maybe you're not such a hard-nose after all, Ella thought.

Of course despite his treatment of Champ, Jacob Weber *had* still left her standing in the entryway rather than offering her a seat in the living room. Which would have been the polite thing to do.

But at that point Ella merely shook her head and remained where she was.

Well, almost.

It was just that the longer she stood there in the narrow entrance with nothing but a steep set of stairs rising up in front of her to study, she became curious about what his place actually looked like. And what it might say about him.

She wasn't brave enough to do any actual snooping, but she did slide a few feet to where the entry merged with the living room, leaning enough to her left to peek into that other section of his house.

She was glad that there weren't any signs of the doctor by then and she assumed he'd gone through the living room into the kitchen that was visible at the other end, at the rear of the town house. But given that brief opportunity, she did take stock of the living room from where she was.

Not that there was much to take stock of.

What little furniture decorated the space appeared expensive and tasteful but there was definitely not much of it. An elaborate oak entertainment center on one wall sported a big-screen plasma television and an impressive stereo system. Directly across from that sat an exquisite overstuffed black leather sofa with a floor lamp to one side and an oak coffee table in front. And that was it. There were no pictures on the walls, no plants to warm up the place, and no other seating. And while the sofa was large enough for more than one person, the room still seemed to be a one-man setup that didn't welcome company.

It made Ella wonder if that was Jacob Weber's own goal—to keep himself removed—or if his off-putting disposition had simply forced him into the role of loner.

The doctor had apparently gone out the back door with the dog because just then Ella heard it open, and the sound of him saying something she couldn't make out gave her fair warning of his return.

She hurriedly straightened up again and sidled to her original position.

He came as far as the living room where she could again hear what he said as he informed Champ that she had her pillow, blanket, bear and monkey to keep her company, instructing her to nap while he was gone and promising treats when he got back.

It was sweet. Maybe more sweet because it was coming from a man who otherwise appeared to be tough as nails, but sweet enough nonetheless to raise Ella's curiosity once again, this time over what exactly lurked behind the man's brusque exterior.

More sounds let her know that he was putting Champ in her crate and within moments of that Jacob Weber was back in the entry with her.

"Is Champ all tucked in for the night?" she asked, pretending she hadn't been privy to any of the doctor's exchange with his pet.

"Not for the night, no. But for the time being, anyway." He raised a big, thick wrist to check the paper-thin watch there and added, "We need to get going."

Ella nodded her agreement, realizing that while Champ may have somehow wormed her way into the doctor's affections and weakened his defenses, talking about Champ didn't soften his demeanor at all.

Maybe nothing did, Ella thought as they left the town house.

Well, fine. If he wanted to keep things purely professional, she'd stop trying to make it anything else and wait for him to begin her orientation.

Which was actually what he did as they set off in the

balmy early-September evening to walk down the street toward the shops that lined the next block.

"The study begins Monday evening," he said without preamble. "Although I won't be there—"

"You won't?" Ella heard herself ask before she'd considered the wisdom—or lack of wisdom—in it. And before she'd had any idea that it would come out in a tone of voice that had a slightly disappointed ring to it. To go along with the disappointed feeling she also discovered in herself…much to her own amazement.

"I'll be there the rest of the time," he was quick to assure her, obviously having caught the tone.

Desperate for damage control, Ella said, "It's just that… I don't know… I guess I thought that since it's your study and your office—"

"It is my study and my office but in essence it will be Dr. Schwartz treating you during this initial phase. My being there at all is really just a courtesy. But I *will* be there. Every night after Monday night."

Ella thought she'd successfully made him believe she'd merely had a moment of patient insecurity, because he continued with what he'd been explaining, only now his voice had a more comforting note to it. "Even though I won't be there Monday night, Marta will be. She'll introduce you to everyone. And Kim Schwartz is not intimidating at all—she's not even five feet tall, weighs about eighty pounds and is very soft-spoken. Very cordial and friendly."

"Good," Ella said, trying to encourage his impression while tamping down on what was really going on with her. Whatever *that* was…

They left the row of town houses and stopped at the corner. As he watched for a break in the cars coming through the intersection, Ella looked ahead at what awaited them on the other side.

They were in an older area of Boston that had been remodeled and updated to attract new residents and businesses. It had been a success because the town houses on either side of the doctor's were occupied and so were all of the storefronts on the next block.

Ella could see a bakery, a bicycle repair shop, a coffee shop, a bookstore, a pizza parlor, a costume shop, and several other small establishments, including their destination at the opposite corner where a neon sign jutting out from the building announced Chicago-Style Hot Dogs.

When they could finally cross, Jacob Weber picked up where he'd left off.

"Marta will be taking some routine, baseline readings on my behalf—blood pressure, pulse, temperature. She'll also take blood and urine so we have labs on you all. Kim—Dr. Schwartz, but she doesn't mind if you call her by her first name—"

"What about you?" For the second time Ella's mouth ran away with her—not something that usually happened.

"What do you want to call me?" he asked, as if challenging her.

Accepting the challenge—and because first names might act as the equalizer she needed with this man, she said, "Jacob. I'll call you Jacob."

Ella had the impression that he considered taking issue with that. But in the end he surprised her by simply conceding, though not without sarcasm.

"Okay. Well, *Ella*, Kim will also be there Monday night," he continued. "She'll have a lot of questions for you—she needs histories as extensive as any other doctor. She'll take your pulse, too, but not for the same purpose that Western medicine does. In Chinese medicine the pulse is taken for the strength and quality of the blood flow. The belief is that it tells something about your chi—your energy. Many practitioners of Chinese medicine base their treatments on that. Kim says she can tell when there are disturbances in the body just from the pulse. She'll also ask to look at your tongue."

Ella glanced over at him, finding his profile as strikingly handsome as the frontal view of his face but trying not to register that fact. "She'll ask to look at my tongue?"

He actually did crack a smile at her reaction. Only a half smile, but a smile nonetheless that softened his features and gave him a whole new appeal as he looked at her, too. "It's a diagnostic tool in Chinese medicine. She's shown me what she looks for and given me the textbook she learned from. I've been using it myself—asking to look at my patients' tongues to see if what I'm finding or suspecting in their physical condition really might be reflected in the way their tongues look. I've found some merit to it. I've also found that after Kim has treated a couple of my patients who went to her on their own—and helped them—that there are changes in the appearance of their tongues. It's actually what prompted this study."

They'd reached the hot-dog stand and although dusk was just beginning to fall, light spilled from the windows in front of it to provide plenty of illumination. Enough so that he said, "I'd rather have better light but let me see yours, anyway."

"You want to examine my tongue out here on the street?"

She couldn't be sure if he was kidding or not. Especially since there was an amused expression on his face.

He glanced around and then said, "Nobody's looking."

The man was too mercurial for her not to worry about refusing him. But they *were* in the open, with several other people milling around them, and Ella knew she would feel like an idiot standing there sticking her tongue out at him. Plus, mercurial or not, there was only so far she was willing to go.

"I will not stick out my tongue," she said firmly.

"You'll have to do it for Kim," he warned gruffly.

"I *will* do it for her. But I *won't* do it for you. Especially not out here."

A passerby looked askance at her just then and Ella realized there might have been some sexual undertones to what she said. Apparently Jacob noticed the same thing, and it obviously amused him because a glint came into his eyes. A very attractive glint that almost seemed to add a certain charm to the man.

But a moment later he glanced away and it was gone.

He opened the door to the hot-dog stand then, once more waiting for her to go in ahead of him.

Ella was only too glad to do it, using the opportunity to tell herself she was out of her mind if she thought this man was capable of being engaging in any way.

He did, however, insist on paying for her hot dog and just as they turned from the register a very small café table in the corner opened up.

"Looks like we get to sit after all," he said, leading her there.

Slathered in mustard, the hot dog tasted great, and as they ate Jacob laid out the course of treatment that would begin on Tuesday evening—when he *would* be in the office, he made sure to remind her.

He reached the end of his orientation at the same time they finished their hot dogs, but he no longer seemed in such a hurry to get this over with. In fact, after pushing away the remnants of his meal, he sat back as if he were surveying her and said, "So how did you become a federal prosecutor? A driving need to put away the bad guys?"

After a moment to register the switched gears and the fact that he was actually making conversation with her, Ella answered him. "Yes, as a matter of fact. That, plus I discovered in law school that I was a good trial attorney. I spent a year in a private firm but after one too many cases defending someone I really believed was guilty—in particular a woman I was reasonably sure had extorted money from an elderly man who had been left penniless as a result—I changed to the other side of the courtroom."

"And your conviction rate?"

"It's high. But it isn't about the numbers for me. If

that becomes the priority, then bad things can happen. Innocent people can go to jail. I don't want that on my conscience. It isn't just a game to me—a competition that my ego has to win—"

"It's about right and wrong. And punishing the evildoers."

"That probably sounds corny to you but yes, that's what it's about to me. If someone does something awful to you or to someone close to you, you want to know they aren't going to get away with it, don't you?"

"Of course."

"But at the same time, what if something happens to point a finger at you for something? For something you didn't do? Do you want to spend years locked up because, as a prosecutor, I refused to look at everything from all sides just to keep my conviction rate up?"

"So, you care."

"Yes, I care."

He nodded, his deep, dark-purple eyes staying on her as if he were seeing past the surface. And maybe even as if he liked what he saw. And heard. Although Ella was wary of going that far.

"What about you?" She wanted to interrupt his study of her. "You must have become a doctor to help people."

"To tell you the truth, no."

"No?" she said with a small laugh, surprised by his answer.

"It was the science I loved. I went into medicine planning to do research, not work with patients."

"How did you end up with patients, then?"

"I didn't at first. I finished medical school and spent

a year in research—like your year defending evildoers rather than putting them away," he said with another of those half smiles she was a little afraid she could get hooked on.

"And you didn't like it as much as you thought you would?" she asked, to urge him on.

"I liked it all right. It was just that during that year I discovered that impregnating mice and rats, and making charts and lists of statistics to write papers from got tedious day after day. I wanted to continue some of the research—like this study in alternative medicine—but I wanted to do it in the real world, with people."

"Where you could see genuine results and not just compile data and end up with paperwork as your final product," Ella guessed.

"Exactly."

"And has it been better for you? Have you enjoyed working with people more than working with rats and mice?"

This time she got a full smile and it doubled the effect. "Don't sound as if you can hardly believe it," he said.

"Did I?" Ella asked, because she honestly hadn't thought it had come out that way.

He only answered her previous question. "Yes, it's been better for me to work with people. I think I've done some good for a lot of them, and if I had spent the last few years in research I'd probably still be doing the same project I started when I graduated from med school."

"I know that from what I've heard and read about

you, you've definitely done some good for a lot of people," Ella confirmed. "That's why I came to see you."

That seemed to remind him of something—maybe that this wasn't a social occasion or that their being together was a professional association—because his smile dissolved, he sat up straighter, and took another look at his watch.

"I'd better get going or I'll be late for this meeting," he said.

Despite the fact that a certain amount of formality had reappeared in him, Ella thought his tone was tinged with what almost sounded like regret to put an end to this.

Still, they both stood and gathered the papers and remnants of their dinners, depositing it all in the trash before leaving the hole-in-the-wall restaurant.

"I appreciate you taking the time to do this for me tonight," Ella said as they headed back up the street. "And dinner was good, too."

That addition made him smile another more-reserved smile, which she caught out of the corner of her eye. "I don't think a hot dog and a bottle of water count as dinner. Don't tell Kim Schwartz that's what I fed you or she'll think I'm sabotaging the study. She's all about balanced everything—a balanced life, a balanced diet, a balanced body."

"She'll probably see it in my tongue on Monday night whether I tell her or not," Ella joked, eliciting a slight chuckle from the imposing doctor and feeling far too pleased with herself that she'd accomplished it.

As they neared his town house and the building directly across from it where his office was, he pointed his chin in the direction of the office building and said, "I can never find a spot to park in front of my place so I use the office lot. Is that where your car is?"

"It is," Ella confirmed.

They crossed the street together and went into the lot where few other cars kept company with the silver Porsche he said was his and the more economical, compact sedan she pointed out as hers.

"I'll walk you to your car," he said, following her to it and waiting for her to unlock the driver's side door.

"Thanks again for the orientation dinner," Ella said, looking up at him from over her open door.

"I'll see you Tuesday night."

"I'll be there," she assured him.

For a moment he just went on standing there, those intense eyes of his staying on her the way they might have had this been the conclusion of a date he didn't particularly want to end.

But then he took a step backward and said, "Drive safely."

"You, too."

He raised his chin to acknowledge that and pivoted on his heels to head for the Porsche.

And as Ella got behind the wheel of her own car and closed the door, she suddenly began to wonder what it might have been like if this *had* been the end of a date. Would he have tried to kiss her?

Kiss her?

Jacob Weber?

That was just too weird to even think about, she told herself as she started the engine.

Too, too weird...

But weird or not, she still couldn't get the idea out of her mind the whole way home.

She also couldn't get out of her mind the lingering and purely baseless thought that it just might have been nice if he had kissed her.

Chapter Four

"Now you're going to let them turn you into a pin-cushion?"

Ella laughed at her sister, Sara's, comment in regards to her announcement that she was about to begin acupuncture treatment for infertility. "Yes, I guess I am," she confirmed.

It was Tuesday and Ella had taken the afternoon off to shop with Sara and Sara's about-to-be-three-year-old daughter, Janey, for Janey's birthday party on Friday night. After buying balloons and streamers and other decorations in the princess theme Janey had chosen, they were at Janey's favorite playground. While Janey climbed on a giant plastic replica of a hamburger, Ella and Sara sat on a bench close by, having mocha lattes.

"It won't only be acupuncture, though." Ella continued to explain her next plan of attack in her attempt to conquer her childlessness. "I met with Dr. Schwartz last night and I'm also taking herbs—a powder form specially blended for me that I mix in water to drink. Plus she'll be teaching us meditation and relaxation techniques and some acupressure, and there's even some therapeutic massage that sounds kind of nice."

"But needles, El, *needles,*" Sara persisted.

"Don't sound so horrified. It isn't as if she's going to poke my eyes out with them or anything. Kim—she's the doctor—showed them to us and they're very, very thin needles, about the width of a hair. They don't go in all that far, either."

"But they do *go* in. Into your skin."

"I'm sure it'll be okay. Acupuncture has been around for centuries—longer than Western medicine. A gazillion people have survived it and I think I will, too."

"I just don't see how that's going to help you get pregnant." Sara added skepticism to her distaste of the idea of the needles.

"It may not. It's an experimental study. That means we're trying something new to see what happens. But one way or another it's harmless. The goal is sort of to reset my body so everything is working the way it should be, to put me at optimal speed so that maybe, when Jacob Weber does in vitro on me again afterward, it will actually take."

"But is it worth it?"

Ella looked over at Janey just as her niece stood tall atop one end of a make-believe stack of toast and leaped off as if it were the accomplishment of a lifetime, laughing gleefully when she landed in the sand.

"Anything—*everything*—is worth it. And believe me, I've been through much worse than being poked with needles," Ella assured her sister.

"Maybe. But have you been through worse than Jacob Weber?" Sara asked.

"I know you never liked him—"

"That's an understatement. No one liked him and most of us actively *dis*liked him."

Ella knew Sara was referring to her college days at Saunders University.

"Maybe you'd feel different if you crossed paths with him now," Ella suggested.

"How could I feel any different when he was such a creep? All those airs he put on. Acting as if it was beneath him to even talk to the rest of us. You know I was in that poli-sci class with him and when the professor broke us up into groups for a project the high-and-mighty Jacob Weber refused to work with us—or with any of the other groups—and instead did an entirely separate project on his own. He made it clear that he'd rather work alone than have to hang out with any of us. It was as if he thought we were lower life forms or something."

Ella had heard that story at the time and on several occasions since—whenever Jacob Weber's name had come up. That was usually because something had been written about him and his accomplishments in a Boston newspaper or in the Saunders University alumni newsletter. But for the first time, Ella felt inclined to refute her sister's opinion of the man. Slightly, anyway.

"To tell you the truth, he kind of surprised me when I was with him on Friday night," Ella ventured tentatively, knowing Sara wouldn't be receptive to hearing anything positive on this subject.

"How did he surprise you? You couldn't believe anyone could be such a big jerk?"

"That was what I thought when I first met him at my consultation and while he kept me waiting in his office on Friday," Ella acknowledged. "But now I don't know, something changed."

"Like what?" Sara asked in disbelief.

"Well, for starters, he has this tiny schnauzer puppy he found on the street when it was only days old and he's been taking twenty-four-hour care of it to keep it alive."

"He probably eats schnauzers with fava beans and a nice Chianti and he's just fattening up the poor thing to make a good meal out of it," Sara said sarcastically.

Ella laughed again but didn't comment on her sister's cutting remark. "Her name is Champ, and he carries her around in his pocket and talks to her like she's a small child. And she seems to love him."

"Give her time."

"No, really, Sara. I'm beginning to think that maybe—just maybe—he isn't all bad. Yes, his social skills leave something to be desired. A lot to be desired. But after a while Friday night he sort of relaxed a little and… I don't know, he was nicer. He can even be funny when he wants to be."

"He's drugged you, hasn't he?"

"Yes, I'm sure there's some kind of make-Jacob-

Weber-easier-to-tolerate medicine in my particular mixture of Chinese herbs," Ella answered facetiously.

"I'm telling you, El, he's the most obnoxious, stand-offish snob I've ever met. Don't be fooled by him because he has a dog."

"It isn't only the dog. He…" Ella struggled to find the words to describe the subtle change she'd seen in the man. "He just got better over time, even after we'd let off the dog. He showed some interest in me as a person, not just as a patient. He asked why I do what I do for a living. He actually listened to what I had to say, and commented and participated in the conversation as if it interested him. He answered my questions about his occupation and why he got into it. We had a nice talk."

"Nice and Jacob Weber? Uh-uh. The two just don't go together. Maybe he's mastered some kind of cloaking device to pull off a better bedside manner," Sara suggested.

"No, his bedside manner is rotten—I saw that when I had my appointment. This wasn't the doctor thing at all. This was actually like seeing the man himself. I'm not sure why it happened—maybe the chemicals in hot dogs have some kind of neutralizing effect on him or something. But I'm telling you that by the end of the time we were together, he wasn't nearly as… As Jacob Weberish."

"Maybe he has plans to eat *you* with fava beans and a nice Chianti."

Ella rolled her eyes. "I'm not saying he didn't start out abrasive and nasty and off-putting, because he did.

I'm just saying that he didn't stay that way. So maybe under the surface—"

"My advice?" Sara said, cutting her off before she could go any further in that vein. "Don't get under *any* surfaces with that guy."

Ella laughed a third time. "You're hopeless."

"What I *hope* is that you're right and he can help you get pregnant," Sara said more seriously as Janey ran to her to show her a pink rock she'd found. "But don't let him fool you into thinking he's a nice guy, because he isn't."

Ella's niece wanted her opinion on the rock, too, and after assuring her it really was beautiful, Ella said to Sara, "The bottom line is that Jacob Weber is the best in his field and that's all that matters."

But that wasn't entirely true.

Because she'd liked it when Jacob had mellowed on Friday night and she hoped that side of him was still in evidence when she saw him again tonight.

And she was afraid that if it wasn't, she was going to be very sorry that it had disappeared.

More sorry than she wanted her sister to know.

Chapter Five

Because Ella was the add-on to the alternative medicine study, her appointment with Dr. Kim Schwartz was scheduled as the last for this and every other evening that treatment was to be administered.

By the time she was finished and in the process of putting her clothes back on, she could hear the sounds of the soft-spoken Chinese doctor, her assistant, and Marta the regular office nurse saying good-night and leaving for the day. Ella assumed that meant that only Jacob would be left, and that unnerved her slightly.

Would it be the awful Jacob or the not-awful Jacob?

There was no way of knowing, since she hadn't so much as seen him tonight to judge his mood, or to predict what his response to her might be after Friday night.

So of course she felt uneasy about the idea of leaving the examining room to find herself alone with him now. It was perfectly reasonable. It had nothing whatsoever to do with having ended up enjoying herself on Friday night. Nothing whatsoever to do with having thought about him almost nonstop since he'd left her in the parking lot. Nothing whatsoever to do with the niggling eagerness she'd discovered in herself every time she'd thought about this office visit and seeing him again. No, it was just that she couldn't be sure what she'd be faced with when it came to him.

Once she was dressed she checked the small mirror on one wall to make sure her mascara wasn't smudged and no stray curls had escaped the scrunchee at her crown. Then she grabbed her purse off the massage table that had replaced the exam table to accommodate the acupuncture, and opened the door.

Jacob was out in the receptionist's area, all right. Across the hall and down several feet, sitting with one hip on the corner of the desk, looking at something in yet another file.

Because the door hadn't made a sound, he didn't seem aware that she was standing there—although if tonight was anything like the beginning portion of Friday night, he could just be ignoring her. But she opted for giving him the benefit of the doubt and for a moment used the opportunity to take in the sight of him.

He was dressed much as he had been both times she'd seen him before—tan slacks, a multicolored plaid shirt and brown tie beneath a sport coat. He looked freshly shaven and it occurred to Ella that if that was the case, it surely didn't have anything to do with her. He probably had another meeting tonight, she thought.

Or maybe even a date.

Why the idea of him having a date disturbed her she didn't know. But she did tamp down that disturbance by reminding herself this was a purely professional relationship. With a man who was more often unlikable than likable. So regardless of what he had planned for the remainder of the evening that had prompted a second shave, she would just say good-night and leave.

And ignore that sinking sensation in the pit of her stomach when she imagined that he was merely waiting for her to get out of there in order to pick up some other woman to take out on the town....

Holding her head high, Ella finally stepped from the doorway of the examining room. Unlike Friday evening, though, that initial movement into the corridor was all it took for Jacob to notice her. And when he did, he immediately stopped what he was doing, closed the file and focused—intently—on her.

"Hi," he said without a bit of warmth in his voice.

Ella returned the simple greeting, wanting to roll her eyes at the return of his bad attitude after it had eased somewhat on Friday night.

"How did you do tonight?" he demanded, setting the closed file on the desk beside him.

"I did pretty well, I think," Ella answered, keeping her own tone cool and aloof. "It was interesting."

Champ was once again in the pocket of Jacob's jacket, and Ella held out her hand to the puppy, addressing her more warmly. "Hello, little Champ. I'm sorry to keep you here so late tonight. You probably have better things to do," she added as if saying that to the dog might garner her information about what Jacob was headed for, despite the fact that she could have kicked herself for being curious.

Neither dog nor doctor said anything to clue her in, however, and as she continued to pet the pup she could feel Jacob's eyes staying on her.

Maybe something was wrong with the way she looked.

She took stock mentally of her own appearance: slip-on shoes, so there were no laces undone; jeans she knew she'd zipped; a plain yellow cardigan sweater buttoned up the front...

No, she was reasonably sure that he wasn't studying her because something was amiss with her clothing. Maybe he was searching for signs of a physical reaction to the acupuncture.

"I'd like to hear the details of the treatment," he said then, sounding as if he were admitting it only reluctantly and breaking the silence but not his steady gaze. "You could give me your impression of Kim, tell me about the experience, what you thought of the acupuncture and how it felt, if you're noticing any aftereffects— things like that."

"Now?" she said, still stuck on the notion that he had a hot date to get to.

"If you have a few minutes." That came out very formally.

She knew he hadn't done this with the other women in the study because while she'd waited her turn for her appointment another woman had come out and asked Marta if there was anything else she needed to do. Marta had said there wasn't, that if the woman had questions for Dr. Weber he would be happy to answer them, but otherwise there was no need to see him. The other woman had merely left the office.

But here he was now, wanting to talk to Ella.

Was that because she was the last patient and he finally had time to spare? Or did he want to talk to her specifically? And if that was the case, was it as a patient or as a person, the way they'd chatted at the end of Friday night?

There were no clues in his expression, and Ella could hardly ask him what was behind the simple request. The simple request that she'd now let go unanswered for an extended period of time.

"Yes. Sure. I mean," she said in a hurry when she realized she was late in answering, "I have a few minutes. Actually, I was just going to ask if I could use your phone to call my sister to come get me—my cell phone is out of commission because my niece ran the battery down playing with it this afternoon, and my car went into the shop for some work today so I'm without wheels. Sara, my sister, dropped me off but couldn't wait, and it'll take her about twenty minutes to come back from her house. I was just going to watch for her downstairs in the lobby, but I can just as easily stay up here in the meantime and tell you whatever you want to know."

Which was much more information than she needed to give.

But Jacob whittled it down. "You need a ride home? How far away do you live?"

"Not far. About two miles. I could walk it but since it's after dark and—"

"Why don't I drive you and we can talk along the way?" he suggested, as if two miles was barely within the parameters he was willing to go.

She hadn't been fishing for that. "You don't have to. I'm sure you were looking forward to going wherever you were going—home or wherever…"

"Champ and I don't have any other plans. We were taking out the car anyway, to grab a burger. It's no big deal to drop you off before we hit a drive-through somewhere."

Nothing like making a woman feel special, Ella thought. Still, she held her annoyance with his attitude in check and said, "A drive-through burger? That's all you were going to do?"

"Yes."

Ella tamped down on the irrational rush of relief that answer sent through her. "How about this, then? I have a casserole in the oven at home. It'll be ready to eat when I get there and there's more of it than I can ever finish. If I accept your ride, you come in and share the casserole."

He didn't jump on that idea, and his hesitation caused her to wonder if she'd overstepped the bounds by inviting him to dinner.

But his hesitation was only momentary before he said, "Sounds great. I can just drop off Champ at—"

"No, Champ can come, too. Unless you don't want to bring her."

"She'll get into mischief," he warned.

Ella reached toward his pocket again and scratched a velvety ear. "How much mischief can anything that small get into?"

"You'd be surprised."

"She can't possibly tear the place up as much as my niece."

"We can hope not, anyway. But I make no guarantees."

"I'm willing to run the risk," Ella said as Champ snuggled against her wrist as if to convince her she was innocent of all accusations.

"It's up to you," Jacob conceded. "Why don't you call your sister and let her know she's off the hook, and we can go?"

Had his sullenness eased up suddenly? Did he actually sound happy to be doing this? Ella thought he did. As happy as she felt. In spite of herself.

"It'll only take a second," she assured.

He pushed away from the desk to allow her free access to the phone—and maybe to give her some privacy—heading toward the rear of the office.

She did manage to get off the phone quickly, though not without another warning from Sara about Jacob, hanging up just as the lights in the rear of the office turned off and Jacob reappeared in the receptionist's area.

"All set?" he asked.

"All set," she confirmed.

There actually wasn't time enough to talk about her acupuncture session during the short drive to her apartment. Ella just gave directions and played with Champ, who rode on her lap.

Then they arrived at her second-floor walk-up and were greeted with the aroma of shepherd's pie baking in the oven.

Jacob didn't have to be told to make himself at home. No sooner were they inside than he shrugged out of his sport coat, removed his tie to stuff in one of the pockets and unfastened the collar button of his shirt.

It was a process that snagged Ella's gaze and did something fluttery to her stomach.

"Champ should have water," she said when he caught her watching him. "I'll get her some."

The apartment wasn't large. The door opened into a space between the living room and the dining area. Her kitchen was just beyond the dining area and behind an island counter that separated it from the living room but allowed her to look out over it. Down a hallway were two bedrooms and a bathroom.

"You can turn on the television while I get things ready, if you want," she informed Jacob from across the island counter as she filled a bowl for the puppy.

"How about if I help you get things ready instead?" he offered, joining her in the kitchen.

Since it was probably better to have him busy than to have him sitting right in front of her where she would be too apt to get lost in looking at him again, Ella accepted the offer. She handed him placemats, plates, napkins and silverware to set the small, round bleached-wood table just outside of her butter-yellow and cobalt-blue kitchen.

While they were each tending to their dinner chores, Champ discovered a ball that Janey had apparently left under Ella's overstuffed blue-and-red sofa. The tiny dog growled and barked and pushed the ball into the dining room.

The ruckus drew the attention of both Ella and Jacob, and the small pup's tenacious attempt to conquer the toy made them laugh.

"Want me to take that away from her?" Jacob asked with a nod in Champ's direction.

"No, she can play with it. I just have a few things here for my niece when she visits, but she isn't really interested in the ball," Ella assured, trying not to think about how nice it was to have someone else there with her, to have the too-cute-to-be-real puppy playing a lively game to entertain them. It was almost familylike and reminded her all over again why she wanted a child so badly. Even if she didn't have a husband to share it with the way she and Jacob had just shared a laugh at Champ.

"Looks like we're all ready," Ella announced after chasing away a hint of longing for this scene to be more than a single, fluke occurrence in her life.

She let Jacob serve himself the French bread she'd sliced and the salad she'd made, but she spooned out the shepherd's pie for him as he sweetened his iced tea.

"So start at the beginning," Jacob said after tasting the casserole and letting her know how good it was. "Tell me what you thought of Kim Schwartz?"

"I really liked her," Ella answered honestly. "Her accent makes her slightly hard to understand sometimes but she doesn't seem to mind repeating things. She's gentle and concerned with my comfort every step of the way, and very kind."

Jacob nodded his handsome head, finished swallowing a bite of food and said, "What about the acupuncture itself? Painful?"

"In some places. I definitely felt the one she put in the side of my little finger and the one in my thumb, but I barely felt the needles that went around my abdomen. And after a few minutes even those that hurt stopped hurting. Then I didn't feel anything at all. And there wasn't any pain taking them out."

"Didn't she have you turn over and do some acupuncture on your back, too?"

"She did."

"What about the needles there?"

"A couple of spots in my back were tense and it was what you'd imagine—a needle going into a knot isn't so comfortable. But for the most part that was the same as the stomach stuff—no big deal. She did cupping, too. Do you know what that is?"

Jacob nodded. "She heats globelike things and sucks them onto your skin."

"Right."

"You'll have bruises from those," he warned.

"I will?"

"Like a whole bunch of hickeys," he said with a mischievous boy's smile. "That was one of the few things we were told about in medical school during our one hour of lecture on alternative medicines. And only so that if we ever got a patient in the emergency room with the marks on them we wouldn't freak out and call Social Services for abuse."

"Will it be that bad?"

He arched an eyebrow. "There'll be bruising. You won't want to wear anything backless for a few days."

"I suppose that's why I feel the way I do after a deep-tissue massage."

"It's more of a workout than it seems it would be," he confirmed. "But all in all? What did you think? Too weird? Too unpleasant?"

"No," Ella answered without having to consider it, and appreciating his interest and what sounded like genuine concern. "Yes, it was strange and there was some minor pain here and there, but on the whole I've had a lot worse done to me in Western medicine procedures."

"And now? How do you feel?"

She felt as if she were enjoying being there with him, talking to him, more than she should be.

But she knew that wasn't what he meant. He wanted to know how she felt *physically.*

"I feel good," she said. "And relaxed. Really relaxed."

Which might account for the sense that she was becoming more and more susceptible to him the longer they were together. At least, she preferred to attribute it to postacupuncture relaxation and not to the possibility that she was developing some sort of attraction to him.

"I'd better do the dishes then," he joked with another of those boyish smiles that made him look ornery and endearing at once.

They'd both finished eating by then but neither of them made a move to leave the table. And apparently she'd told him all he wanted to know about her experience with Chinese medicine because when Champ lost interest in the ball and came to whine at his side to be lifted onto his lap, he changed the subject.

"I got to thinking about it while you were on the office phone to your sister—I might have gone to college with a Sara Gardner. That *is* what you said your sister's name is, right? Sara?"

"Right. Well, Sara Gardner was her name when she was at Saunders. She's Sara Wirth now," Ella said, confirming that he and her sister had been in the same class at the university.

One of his well-shaped eyebrows rose again. "Did you know I went to school with your sister?"

"She remembered you." *Just please don't remember anything about me....*

"And you didn't bring it up?"

"Sara didn't think you would know who she was so I thought there was no point." *And I didn't want to risk stirring memories of what you might have heard when it came to me.*

"Your sister's name rang a bell, but to tell you the truth I probably wouldn't be able to recognize her on the street," he admitted. "What about you? Where did you get your undergrad degree?"

It wasn't a question Ella was thrilled to be asked. But there was no way not to answer it. "I went to Saunders, too. A little ahead of you and Sara."

He looked perfectly comfortable sitting across from

her in the ladder-back chair, one big hand slowly, tenderly stroking the puppy now asleep in his lap. Had Ella not been so worried that he was going to recall the scandal that had swirled around her at the end of her college career, she would have been thinking more than peripherally about what it might feel like to have that hand stroking her.

But as it was, she was suddenly more on edge than aroused. Which was probably a good thing, she told herself. Even if it didn't seem that way.

She held her breath, waiting for things to click in his mind, waiting for him to put two and two together, to realize that Sara wasn't the only Gardner whose name he might have heard around Saunders University.

"What about Gilbert Harrison—remember him?" Jacob asked then.

He does know! Ella silently lamented.

But she kept a tight hold over herself and said, "Of course I remember Professor Harrison."

Here it comes....

"Have you heard that the board is after him? That they're trying to have him fired?"

It took a moment to sink in that Jacob was talking about something other than Ella's history at Saunders. That even though he was referring to Gilbert Harrison, it wasn't in reference to her.

"Professor Harrison?" she repeated. "The board is trying to oust him?"

"They are. The president of the college board of directors, Alex Broadstreet, in particular."

"Why?" Ella asked, her own surprise taking over her

personal concerns. "Professor Harrison was—and I'm sure still is—a good man. He went above and beyond the call of duty to help students. Selflessly. In more ways than... Well, in more ways than any other professor or advisor or administrator."

And she'd gone overboard in her accolades and fervor. She could tell by the fact that both of Jacob's eyebrows were arched now.

"Sounds like you have firsthand knowledge."

If Jacob didn't know about her troubles at Saunders, she didn't want to expose herself. And there were other reasons why she couldn't go into all she knew about exactly how good a man Gilbert Harrison was, so she consciously toned it down.

"I know he doesn't deserve to lose his job," she said strongly. "How can that even be a possibility?"

"The board claims he's too old-fashioned," Jacob said. "Students go to him with their problems and he fights for them. They hang out in his office, consider him a friend and ally—"

"Because that's what he is."

"Well, the board doesn't want him being such a pal to the students. They want more decorum. What I think they really want is someone new in there who will let them call all the shots without questioning them, someone who doesn't mind being the board's puppet. But they're claiming that there have always been rumors surrounding Gilbert and his relationship with some of the students—not like accusations of sexual misconduct or anything, but that he's done some *scheming,* as they call it, on students' behalf. And Broadstreet is determined to get to the bottom of everything and anything to do with Gilbert. Basically they're just determined to find a reason to fire him."

"That's awful. It just can't happen. It shouldn't be *allowed* to happen."

"We're doing all we can to stop it but—"

"Who's we?" Ella interrupted him to ask.

"A group of his students. He also advised many of us. David and Sandra Westport, Kathryn Price, Nate Williams, and Rachel James, along with me."

"Nate Williams—I know him."

"From Saunders?"

"No, actually I didn't know him there. I didn't even know that was where he went to school. He's a defense attorney, and I've faced him several times in court. Some of the other names are vaguely familiar from college, but I don't know any of them. Except you. How did you all find out about this and decide to help?"

"It was at Gilbert's request. He chose some of his former students—me among them—and asked us to do what we can to make the board back down. We're all giving depositions that essentially testify to the fact that he's only done good things for us, and never acted inappropriately on our behalf. Which in my case—like maybe in yours—is true enough."

Jacob had added the *like maybe in yours* with a question in his tone, letting her know he suspected she, too, had a history with Gilbert Harrison. And the expectant look he was leveling on her now made her think he was hoping she might enlighten him as to what that history was.

But that wasn't going to happen. After all, he hadn't told her what Gilbert had done for him, so why should she be any more forthcoming?

When she wasn't, Jacob continued anyway. "Unfortunately, Gilbert isn't doing all that much to help himself."

"He isn't tooting his own horn even as a defense?"

"No, he isn't. And we don't know why. We're doing what we can to support him, to get the board to let him keep his job and keep doing what he's done for the students all along, but it's proving to be a rough road. And with this closemouthed attitude of his, we're trying to find anything and anyone who can aid the cause on his behalf." Jacob hesitated, then looked Ella in the eye. "Is there a chance your sister or you know anything or have some experiences of your own that might work in Gilbert's favor?"

What Ella knew she couldn't tell.

And yet it tore her up to think of sitting idly by, doing nothing to repay the man who had saved her neck and made her entire future possible.

So, without revealing anything she shouldn't, she said, "I know Sara never had any dealings with Professor Harrison, but I'd like to do whatever I can. I'd be happy to be a character witness or sign a petition or start a campaign of some kind—letter writing or whatever you need."

"I'm not exactly sure what you can do, but it might just lend some weight to Gilbert's defense to have a federal prosecutor in his corner."

"True. Since I go after bad guys for a living, if I'm

convinced he isn't one of them, maybe that could knock some wind out of the board's sails."

"The group is meeting on Thursday night, after I finish at the office. Why don't you come with me? I'll introduce you to everyone and see if somebody doesn't have a thought about something you can do."

And that meant she would get to have another evening with him....

Ella wasn't quite sure why *that* was the first thing to pop into her head. Except that once again she'd enjoyed their time alone together and so certainly wasn't dreading the opportunity to see him again.

"I'd really like to," she said. Then, afraid she'd sounded overeager to spend more time with him in a not-professional setting, she qualified her agreement. "I'd like to do whatever I can to help Professor Harrison."

"Great. Then it's a date."

Was it a date? Or was that just an offhand remark that didn't mean anything?

Ella wasn't sure. But she *was* sure that she shouldn't have been so thrilled to think even for a minute that Thursday night might actually be a date....

Jacob glanced at the schoolhouse clock on the dining room wall then and said, "I should get going and let you rest."

"I'm fine. I feel wonderful—"

Ella cut herself short, hating that the words had spilled out on their own again, that they'd made it clear she wasn't anxious to have him go.

To counteract the impression, she said, "But you—

and Champ—have had a long day. I'm sure you want to get home."

Jacob smiled a small smile that left her wondering if he'd seen through her. But still he picked up the sleeping puppy in one hand and stood.

"Let me hold her while you put on your coat," Ella suggested, reaching for the puppy who barely roused even when Jacob moved her.

Ella cuddled her, watching Jacob only out of the corner of her eye as he slipped his long arms into his sport coat and settled it around the broad, straight shoulders she didn't want to admire as much as she did.

When he was ready for Champ, Ella rubbed her own nose to one ear and handed her back.

Jacob raised the pup to his face, almost nose to nose, "You're down for the count tonight, aren't you, little girl?" he said with a laugh before lowering her to his expansive chest where the puppy rested her head as if it were a pillow made specifically for her comfort.

A comfort Ella felt surprisingly envious of as the urge to lay her own head against Jacob's chest struck from out of nowhere.

She took a deep breath to chase away the unwanted and unwarranted thoughts and led the way to her apartment door.

"Thanks for the ride home," she said as he followed her.

"Thank *you* for dinner," he said, stopping in the doorway rather than going completely into the hall. "And for the company," he added more softly and with a smile so sexy Ella actually felt as if her blood heated a few degrees.

His deep, dark-blue eyes stayed on her, but there was suddenly something different in the way he was looking at her. Something that had nothing to do with a doctor-patient relationship. Something that was clearly and solely the look of a man taking in the sight of a woman.

And maybe liking what he saw as much as she liked what she saw as she stood there gazing up at him, too.

At those nearly purple eyes, at that shockingly handsome face made all the more amazing by his engaging expression that softened some of those sharp angles and lines.

Then one corner of his mouth drifted upward and he leaned forward to kiss her. A quick-as-lightning kiss that brought his mouth into contact with hers so faintly it was almost as if he hadn't kissed her at all.

"Good night," he said then, his smile broader and pleased.

With himself? With her? With the kiss or the fact that even though she hadn't had time to actually kiss him back, she also hadn't backed away from it or slapped him because of it?

Ella didn't know.

"Good night," she answered, sounding as stunned and confused as she felt.

But stunned and confused and shocked and definitely thrown off-kilter by the fact that the impressive and imposing Dr. Jacob Weber had kissed her were nothing in comparison with the other thing she felt when he'd left and she closed the door.

Because along with being stunned and confused and

shocked and thrown off-kilter, she felt sort of sparkly inside.

And even though the acupuncture might have caused some aftereffects she wasn't expecting, she was sure the sparkly feeling came completely from liking that the doctor had, indeed, kissed her.

Chapter Six

When her telephone rang at seven-thirty the next morning, Ella didn't have to answer it to know who it was. Her sister was the only person who ever called that early. So, as she stood at her kitchen counter eating a piece of toast before leaving for her office, she picked up the receiver and said, "Hi, Sara."

"Oh, good, you're still alive."

Ella laughed, knowing her sister was being facetious. "Alive and kicking."

"Even after having needles stuck in you and then being driven home by Jacob Weber?"

"As hard as it might be to believe, it's the truth."

"I really wouldn't have minded coming back to pick you up," Sara said.

"I know, but he offered and it seemed silly not to just take him up on it."

"So give me the gory details," Sara ordered.

"About the acupuncture or the drive home?"

"Start with the acupuncture and then get to the bad part."

Between bites of toast, Ella filled her sister in on the details of her first experience with Chinese medicine, leaving out the fact that she had ended up with bruises on her back, because they sounded worse than they felt, and making the entire procedure seem like a breeze so as not to alarm the overly alarmable Sara.

"It doesn't seem too horrible," Sara said when Ella had finished.

"It wasn't horrible at all," Ella insisted, meaning it. "In fact, it was a whole lot more humane and—I don't know, more organic, maybe—than any Western medicine procedure I've suffered through in the past three years. And I think I slept better than I ever have in my life. That seemed like an added bonus."

When she'd finally managed to fall asleep, anyway. It had taken her until nearly 2:00 a.m. to get there because her mind had been racing between thoughts of her old English professor's problems and that kiss Jacob had given her at the door. That little nothing-of-a-kiss that had somehow managed to linger in her mind a billion times longer than it had in real life.

"I'm glad the acupuncture was good," Sara said then. "Now get to the bad part."

"Being driven home by Jacob wasn't bad," Ella said, easing into that news because she knew it wasn't what her sister wanted to hear. "It was actually nice. He stayed for dinner, his puppy played with one of Janey's balls, and we had an altogether good time. A really, really good time."

"Boy, does he have you fooled!"

"Or you," Ella countered. "All I know is that when he wants to, he can be a perfectly pleasant, interesting man."

"You aren't seeing him as a challenge or something, are you, El? A project? A feather in your cap if you can win him over and humanize him and be the one woman he falls for?"

"No, I don't see him as any of those things. And I'm not looking to change any man or win anyone over. I've had two evenings with Jacob that have involved stimulating conversation, and that's the extent of it. But stimulating conversation is hardly cause for condemnation, either."

"'Jacob'…that's the second time you've called him that."

"It's his name," Ella said without making apologies for her use of it. "That's what I call him when I'm not calling him darling or sweetheart or lovebug."

That accomplished what she'd intended: Sara laughed and lightened up. "I'd pay a lot of money to see someone call Jacob Weber lovebug."

"Well, start saving up," Ella advised with a laugh of her own. Then she toned it down and changed the subject. "I'm glad you called, though. I have a dilemma I need help with."

"A dilemma that involves Jacob Weber?"

"No, Sara, we're done talking about Jacob Weber. My dilemma is about something else entirely. It's a decision I have to make that has moral and ethical implications, and I don't know what to do. But you're good at things like this, so I want to run it past you."

"Is this a case you're working on or something personal? Is there any kind of client-attorney privilege involved?"

Ella smiled at the sound of the wheels of her sister's mind turning. Sara loved being a stay-at-home mom, but Ella knew her sister sometimes yearned for more complicated mental exercise.

Still, Ella didn't want to give away too much and so only said, "There's no client-attorney privilege in place or I wouldn't be talking to you about it."

Sara didn't seem to notice that Ella had left the remainder of her questions unanswered because she said, "Okay, shoot."

Ella took a deep breath. "A long time ago I accidentally found out something about someone. And that someone made me swear never to tell."

"Something they did that was illegal?"

"Yes…maybe…well, I don't know. Something kind that they didn't have to do. They just didn't want it known, and because this person had done something important to help me, I was indebted, so I agreed to keep the secret. Not that I would have told the secret, anyway, because it was really none of my business and I had no reason *not* to keep the secret, but the point is, I promised never to tell anyone."

"And obviously you never have, because I don't have

any idea what you're talking about, and if you were going to tell anyone, it would have been me," Sara said, confident that that was true.

"Right," Ella confirmed.

"But now you *do* want to tell someone," Sara guessed.

"Well, now that person is in major trouble, trouble they shouldn't be in, and they're being treated unfairly, and if what I know about them came to light, it might help them get out of the situation."

"Then why wouldn't this someone use what you know to defend themselves?" Sara reasoned.

"They're acting under an old promise of their own to someone else to keep this quiet, and I'm assuming they're sticking to it even though sticking to it makes their situation more difficult. But given that, should *I* tell the secret and help the person out?"

"Hmm," Sara mused.

"I told you it was a dilemma."

"Wrapped in a conundrum and tied with a quandary."

And that was without Sara knowing that to reveal the secret could also reveal Ella's own best-kept secret. Something her sister didn't know about her because she'd been too ashamed to let even her family in on it. But she had no doubt that if she so much as mentioned that portion of her problem, Sara wouldn't rest until she heard every last, unsavory detail.

"So what would you do if you were in my shoes?" Ella asked. "Would you break the confidence and tell the secret to help? Or figure that if the person is so determined to keep the secret, I should go on keeping it, too?"

"Will telling the secret hurt someone else?" Sara asked.

"Well, I guess it could prove that the person showed favoritism. But I don't think that does a *lot* of harm. It's more that I'd be going against the explicit wishes of this person, and breaking my word to them." To someone who had helped her and asked only this in return.

"Okay, let's review and make sure I have it all straight," Sara said as if she'd heard enough to make her decision. "Revealing the secret would help this person and hurt no one?"

"Right."

"And as far as you know, this person is keeping the secret because they promised someone else—who also wouldn't be hurt—that they wouldn't tell?"

"Right."

"And telling the secret really could do the person some good, and the person doesn't deserve what's happening to them and *does* deserve to be saved?"

"Right."

"Then I guess I'd say that for this person's own good, you should tell the secret," Sara concluded. "Even if it makes them mad that you do."

And even if it exposed the one thing about Ella that she'd hoped no one would ever find out about?

It was Ella's turn to say only, "Hmm…"

"You don't agree?" Sara asked.

"I don't *dis*agree. It's just complicated. And I hate to break my promises."

"But how will you feel if you don't do it and something bad comes of not doing it?" Sara reasoned.

"I'll feel rotten," Ella said. But even so, she still wasn't completely convinced that she should do it. "I guess I'll have to think about it some more."

"Well, do it without the company of Jacob Weber, would you?" Sara said, returning to what seemed to have become her pet peeve.

"I'm in his company every night when I go to his office for these treatments," Ella reminded her sister, omitting the fact that she already had plans to see him after Thursday's appointment, too. And that she was looking forward to it. A lot.

Instead she said, "I have to go or I'll be late for work. Thanks for playing sounding board and kiss Janey for me."

"I will. And let me know what you decide about your dilemma."

"When I solve it," Ella said.

But even if she did opt for revealing the secret she'd been carrying for so many years, she wasn't sure she'd let her sister in on it.

Not when she knew it would mean telling Sara the whole story.

The whole story about how and why she'd come to learn the secret in the first place.

As Jacob slipped into the private door of his office that evening he could hear Kim Schwartz's voice still coming from his waiting room.

"Good, we made it in time," he whispered to Champ,

who was riding in his suit coat pocket as he closed the door behind him and turned on the light that illuminated his desk.

He scooped the tiny dog out of his pocket and put her on the floor, then crossed to the sofa to set down the purpose and product of his errand.

Tonight the group doing the alternative medicine study had initially met Dr. Schwartz all at once. She was teaching them how to meditate and then planned to meet with each patient individually to show them which acupressure points to use to support their particular course of acupuncture treatment.

Jacob had looked in at the beginning of the group session but had left when he'd given in to something he'd been trying all day long to talk himself out of.

Since his inner-office door was open to the corridor, he saw Kim Schwartz step from the waiting room into the hallway, leading the first of the group back to one of the examining rooms to begin the individual acupressure lessons.

That meant he didn't have long, so he crossed to the inside door and closed it to prevent Champ from wandering out while his attention was elsewhere. Then he took off his suit coat, hung it in the closet and went into his private bathroom for a quick shave; he kept an electric razor there for late-day or last-minute spruce ups.

As he stood in front of the mirror running the buzzing appliance over his face, he wondered what the hell had gotten into him to be planning a way to spend time alone with Ella Gardner again tonight when Kim Schwartz was finished with her.

Planning?

Plotting was more like it.

Plotting to catch Ella before she could leave. Plotting what he'd say about the dinner he'd just made a mad dash to get for them. Plotting the reason he would give for it.

So what the hell *had* gotten into him? he asked himself, still slightly surprised that he hadn't been able to conquer the crazy urge to do this tonight.

Curiosity was one of the things that had gotten into him. He was curious about Ella's connection and obvious loyalty to Gilbert Harrison, about why she felt so strongly about helping her former English professor. He knew *he* had a good reason for lending a hand to Gilbert when he hadn't seen or talked to the man in ten years, but he wanted to know why Ella would. Why she was so determined to.

He was curious about it all even though it wasn't any of his business. He was curious about it all even though he hadn't been intrigued by the whys or wherefores of anyone else he'd been working with on Gilbert's behalf.

But as he shaved the left side of his face he refused to think too much about that lack of interest in anyone else's motives and stubbornly stuck with the fact that he was doing what he was doing now because he was curious about what was spurring Ella. Somehow that seemed to make it more acceptable.

If he could avoid looking at it too closely.

And then, too, he also needed to tell her that he'd checked with the rest of the alumni working on Gilbert's case—most of them, anyway—and that they were open to her coming with him on Thursday night and doing whatever she could for the cause.

Of course, telling her about Thursday night didn't require his trip to the gourmet food market down the street where he'd dished out a ridiculously inflated amount of cash for one of their specials—a wicker basket that contained a complete picnic supper for two. He could merely stop her before she left and inform her that she'd gotten the go-ahead for the meeting.

But again it gave him what could be construed as a reason for what he had in the works.

A reason that wasn't merely that he liked her. That he found her fun to be with. And relaxing and entertaining and amusing and illuminating. And arousing...

Because those reasons were much harder for him to admit to, despite the fact that they were true. Acting on those reasons alone would make him feel weak and vulnerable. And weak and vulnerable were not things he liked to feel, he thought as he completed his shave and turned off the razor.

So here he was, feeling like a nerdy kid about to make sure he encountered the cute girl up the street so he could walk her to school as if it was purely by happenstance.

Happenstance with an expensive picnic basket.

And even if he could pass this off as a chance encounter, how was that better? he demanded of himself disgustedly, thinking that this might be the lamest thing anyone had ever done. Certainly it was the lamest thing *he'd* ever done.

So maybe he shouldn't do it....

He put away the shaver and gave his reflection a hard stare in the mirror.

"It isn't too late to back out," he said.

But he knew he wasn't going to.

Because backing out would mean that he would exchange a few words with Ella just before she left the office and be left to pack up Champ, walk across the street to his town house and sit alone for the rest of the night. Thinking about Ella. The way he always seemed to be thinking about her lately.

Thinking about her and wishing things no woman had ever made him wish before.

Wishing just to hear her voice.

Wishing to see the way light played in the twists and turns of that curly hair of hers.

Wishing to talk to her and hear her view on things.

Wishing for her company and the sound of her laughter and the soft scent of her perfume.

Wishing simply to be with her.

And he knew he'd be wishing it all so much that he'd regret not going through with even a lame attempt to accomplish it. For whatever the reasons.

Champ discovered him in the bathroom just then, clamped her teeth onto his pant leg and began to wrestle with it as if the tiny schnauzer could topple him if she tried hard enough.

Jacob bent over and picked her up in one hand, holding her so he could look her in the eye.

"Maybe letting you sleep in my bed has infected me with some kind of parasitic insanity," he said to Champ, who unabashedly bit his nose in response.

"Ouch!" he exclaimed, rearing out of the little dog's reach to prevent her from doing it again. "I let you get close and you bite me? Bad girl," he chastised firmly, trying to keep from laughing at the fact that Champ was wagging her tail merrily.

But as he set her on the floor again it occurred to him that maybe the puppy's nip was a warning to him. A warning that letting Ella get too close could end up getting him metaphorically bitten just the way letting Champ get close when she was in this mood had.

Warning or not, though, he still couldn't force himself to scratch the plan he'd set into motion for tonight.

But it was just tonight, he promised himself.

Well, tonight and tomorrow night.

Then he *would* back off to make sure she *didn't* get too close.

The same way he did with other women.

The way he always had.

To keep them at a distance.

But oddly, for the first time in his life, that thought didn't give him the sense of control it usually did.

It might even have given him something that resembled a sense of sadness.

But that was ridiculous, he told himself, as he left the bathroom with Champ following behind.

He didn't get sad about things like not having a woman or anyone else in his life. Not anymore. He'd overcome that a long, long time ago—when he'd learned it was better to be on his own and self-sufficient.

"So tonight and tomorrow night, and then that's it,"

he said, as if saying it aloud made it an irrevocable declaration.

But mostly he was thinking that at least he *had* tonight and tomorrow night....

Chapter Seven

"You can mix a small amount of water with the herbs and drink it very fast if the taste is too bad."

The advice came from Kim Schwartz in her partially broken English. Ella had waited her turn to see the pretty Asian doctor alone after learning to meditate. The diminutive woman, who exuded health and energy, had shown Ella where and how to apply acupressure. Once Kim Schwartz was convinced Ella knew what to do, she escorted her out of the examining room to the nurse's work area. There Kim gave Ella the second bottle of Chinese herbs she'd specially blended for her, warned her that these were less palatable than the first batch, and advised her on how to help avoid the taste.

Ella counted out four measures of the spoon included with the herbs, stirred it into a little warm water and even though not all of it mixed very well, she threw it back as if it were a shot of whiskey.

It didn't help the taste. Or the texture.

But the face she made afterward caused Kim to smile. "I know, not nice. But they're good to take anyway."

Ella put effort into smoothing out the grimace she knew was on her face, rinsed the paper cup she'd used and tried to wash down the sandy herbs that were still sticking to her tongue and the back of her throat.

"Two times a day. Morning and night, along with the others," Kim Schwartz dictated before bidding her good-night and heading out of the office.

Ella waited until the doctor was out of sight but couldn't contain another, more animated grimace as she attempted to clear her throat.

"That bad?"

Jacob had come around the corner into the work station at just the right moment, catching Ella in the act of making her facial critical review of the herbs.

She was so unreasonably happy to see him, though, that she managed to turn on a smile instead.

"No, not so bad," she lied to trick him. "I think you ought to try a little to see for yourself."

The answering grin on his handsome face was worth the untruth despite the fact that he obviously saw through it.

"Not a chance," he responded. "Kim says the herbs are the biggest complaint she gets from her patients."

"I don't know why," Ella deadpanned. "My first bottle had some spices in the mix and this blend tastes like a dusty old antique store smells. And in the new ones," Ella continued, "you get lots of lovely grit and sand and sawdustlike stuff. Mmm-mm-good!"

Jacob laughed, creating some very sexy lines at the corners of his eyes and equally appealing grooves down his cheeks.

Then he poked a thumb over his shoulder in the direction of his inner office. "I have some dinner and fruit-flavored tea that might help wash it down, if you're interested."

Ella wasn't quite sure what that meant. Was he offering her a bite of his food or a sip of his drink to get the bad taste out of her mouth in lieu of a mint or a piece of gum, maybe?

Confused, she opted for what she considered a safe response. "I couldn't take any of your dinner. Just a little more water is all I need," she said, filling her glass again and drinking it as Jacob surprised her by looking almost sheepish.

"Actually," he countered, sounding that way, as well, "I just went out and got dinner for two. I thought I could pay you back for feeding me last night. Unless you have other plans...."

So he was inviting her to have dinner with him?

Ella's confusion mounted. If he wanted her to have dinner with him again tonight why hadn't he just asked? Or was that what he thought he was doing now and had just botched it?

She couldn't figure it out. But as he stood there—the indomitable Dr. Weber—with even a hint of uncertainty about him, she couldn't help thinking that whatever he was doing, there was something endearing about the fact that he *wasn't* so sure of himself for once.

Plus, when it came to the chance to spend time with him again, she found herself all too willing to jump at it. In spite of knowing she shouldn't.

"My only plans for dinner were a sandwich and a salad at home in front of the television tonight," she said before giving more thought to those "shouldn't" reasons that might persuade her to say no.

Jacob's expression turned purely pleased. "Great. Come on back and we'll see what's in this basket I bought."

He led her to his inner office where Champ was standing on her hind legs, her paws braced as high up on the front of the sofa as she could manage, craning her head toward a picnic basket beyond her reach.

A picnic basket?

Ella didn't know what she'd expected to find as the meal Jacob had brought in for them—a bucket of fried chicken, maybe—but she certainly hadn't expected a picnic, complete with a wicker basket. He had to have put a lot of thought into this and gone to some trouble to do it.

As if he could tell what was going through her mind and felt compelled to disabuse her of those notions, he said, "There's a market that just opened down the street. I wanted to try a variety of what they're selling, and this seemed to be my chance to do it. And I figured I could use the basket to cart Champ and some of her stuff back and forth."

Ella got the message—he didn't want her to believe

what he had here was a romantic dinner for two. But no matter what kind of spin he put on it, that's exactly what this was. And, heaven help her, she was thrilled with it. With him for coming up with the idea and acting on it.

But she didn't give him any clue that she wasn't buying his excuse. Not since this whole thing seemed to have unnerved him so much.

"What do you say to sitting on the floor?" Jacob said then. "We can eat off the coffee table."

"Okay," Ella agreed, going with the this-is-all-no-big-deal illusion he clearly wanted to maintain.

As she set her purse beside the couch, he moved the visitors' chairs closer to the desk to give them more room. He also confounded Champ when he lifted the tiny puppy to the couch cushion but removed the picnic basket she'd been working so hard to get to, setting it on the floor.

Champ barked to register her complaint but could only lie down with her paws and head just over the edge of the sofa to look longingly at what remained out of her reach since she was too tiny to jump from the couch.

"Poor Champ," Ella cooed, petting the puppy. "She wants what's in that basket so bad."

"What she'd really like is to get inside it and have first crack at everything," Jacob said, laughing.

Ella sat on the floor then, on one side of the coffee table, bracing her back against the couch front, while Jacob took up position just around the corner of the table so he was facing her.

It occurred to Ella that she was dressed more for an

informal picnic supper on the floor than he was. Before coming here tonight she'd changed from her work clothes into jeans and a boat-neck T-shirt, but Jacob had on suit pants and a beige dress shirt, which even without a tie and with the collar button unfastened and the sleeves rolled to his elbows, still weren't floor-sitting attire.

But he didn't seem to care as he pulled food from the basket and read the labels to her as he set it out.

"Looks like we have a small wheel of brie with spiced apples and cranberries to eat on crackers. Croissant sandwiches—turkey, smoked gouda, lettuce, tomato and avocado with chipotle mayonnaise. Red potato salad. Multicolored pasta salad with a kalamata olive dressing. A minivegetable tray. And coconut-macadamia-nut bittersweet chocolate chip cookies for dessert."

"Wow," Ella marveled.

"It all sounds good?"

"It all sounds great. I'm getting hungrier with every description," she assured.

He also took plates, silverware, napkins and bottles of fruit tea from the basket.

"So how did tonight go—with the exception of the herbs?" he asked as they began with the brie and crackers.

"It went well. The meditation makes you feel like you're floating, and the acupressure won't be difficult to do. It seems too simple to have any real effect, but Kim says people can be successfully treated for a lot of things using only that."

"That's what she tells me, too," Jacob confirmed.

They moved on from the brie to the rest of the meal and for a while they focused on the food, sampling everything, judging it all and taking more of what they liked best.

Then, as they settled into simply eating and sharing a morsel now and again with Champ, Jacob said, "I got you the go-ahead for the meeting tomorrow night—if you're still interested."

Gilbert Harrison and his problems hadn't been far from Ella's mind since Jacob had told her what was going on, so she knew exactly what he was talking about. Not to mention that before this picnic supper she'd thought the meeting Thursday night would be her next opportunity to be with Jacob and she'd been fighting her own inclination to be excited about that all day.

"I'm glad," she said. "I meant it when I told you I want to do whatever I can to help."

"It might help to know why that is," he said nonchalantly.

So he was still wondering what had inspired her loyalty to her old college teacher, and tonight he'd decided to probe a little. But Ella hadn't decided yet just how much she was willing to reveal, so she ignored the comment and instead said, "Those of you who Professor Harrison chose to fight for him must have been very close to him."

"I can't speak for the others, but I wasn't, no. In fact, you couldn't say that I jumped at the chance to help out."

"You didn't? Why not?"

He shrugged one big, broad shoulder. "Well, at first

Gilbert just asked me to meet with him. I thought he was probably on some kind of fund-raising committee and wanted money, so I sent a check and left it at that. But he kept after me until I finally drove out to the university and talked to him."

"But then, when you heard what was going on, you decided to do what you could for him, too."

Jacob didn't confirm that readily. He finished his sandwich and seemed to mull over her comment, leaving her wondering why.

After a moment he took a deep breath, sighed it out, and said, "No. I still had to do some soul searching before I got onboard. I didn't really want to get into anything that had to do with my past or with the years I was at Saunders. Those weren't good times for me, and Gilbert was essentially calling in a favor that brought it all back, so I dragged my feet."

"Until?"

"Until I realized that a debt is a debt, and I owed Gilbert one."

His handsome face had sobered into an expression serious enough to make Ella wonder if she'd opened a door to a lot of old demons. But how could that be? How could Jacob's past or his years at Saunders *not* have been good times?

"Are you trying to tell me that the school's most notorious rich kid didn't play and party hardier than anybody?" she asked.

He cast her a sad-looking smile. "The school's most notorious rich kid?"

"That was you," she reminded him.

He laughed, but there was bitterness in his tone. "It was a sham."

That sounded like a confidence but still Ella found it difficult to believe. "What was a sham?" she demanded.

"Everything. My home life for starters."

"Life with Mom and Dad in the mansion wasn't all we lesser mortals thought it was?" Ella said skeptically.

"It wasn't life with Mom and Dad in the mansion," he said. "That's just how I tried to make it appear. The truth was much different. Much, much different."

"How?" Ella ventured, not sure she was going to get away with it.

But Jacob didn't shoot her down. He was finished with his meal and pushed his plate away as she'd done several minutes before. Then he braced his forearms on the coffee table and said, "The truth is that my father took off when I was twelve. With all of what was left of the family funds after he and my mother had basically blown the fortune my grandfather had made in textiles. I never saw or heard from dear old Dad again, and I don't have any idea if he's living or dead to this day."

"You're joking," Ella said in shock.

"No, I'm not."

"Was this something a lot of people knew and I just didn't, or—"

"No one knew. My mother told people my father was traveling, or working in Europe to explain why he was never there, and since she was rarely there either, by the time I was fourteen, she didn't have to worry about any-body questioning her too closely."

"Where did she go when you were fourteen?"

"She didn't completely disappear—the way my fa-ther did—but almost. She had income from a small trust fund of her own—just enough to keep up the pre-tenses—plastic surgery to make sure she looked good, expensive clothes, the first-class airfare to fly off for ex-tended visits to wealthy friends where, once she was there, it didn't cost her anything to live but insured she was in good standing with her social circle. She'd show up at home two or three times a year—usually for a lit-tle nip-tuck recovery, as she liked to call it, and then she'd be gone again."

"So you were raised by servants?"

He laughed a humorless laugh. "Servants? There weren't any servants. The house was built by my grand-father so it wasn't mortgaged, and my mother did man-age to pay the taxes on it—probably because to have the government confiscate it would have blown her cover. But other than that there was barely money to pay utilities—which sometimes happened instead of my being able to buy food. Winters I did all my living in the smallest room with a fireplace so I could burn what-ever wood I could chop myself to keep the heating bill low. I was just lucky to not have the electricity and wa-ter turned off and the furnace going only enough for the pipes not to freeze."

The level of his voice had risen and grown heated, angry, bitter. Ella thought that what she was seeing was the origin of what had made him into the man before her now. "You didn't even have food? From when you were fourteen?" she asked, amazed.

"I fended for myself," he said as if he liked the sound of that better. "I lied about my age and got hired at the grocery store within walking distance of my house. I guess nobody expected one of the Boston-elite Webers to be looking for work, so they didn't seem to put two and two together to figure out who I was. Plus my job was to stock shelves overnight and the night crew I was teamed with wasn't a close-knit bunch. We all just came in, did our jobs and clocked out. Which was exactly how I wanted it. And as an extra, added bonus, I got to take home food that was slightly moldy or had reached expiration dates or was too damaged to be sold."

"And then you went to school during the day?"

"Right."

"When did you sleep?"

"After school, before my shift started. It was good training for residency."

"And you never told someone—anyone—that you were on your own, eating moldy food, at fourteen? Not a school counselor? Or a teacher? Or a friend's parent? A person who could help you?"

He laughed another wry, mirthless laugh. "My family's name is on a wing at the university. How could I go to anyone and say that yes, my grandfather had made enough money that we should all have been well taken care of forever, that he'd been a generous contributor to Saunders, to the whole city of Boston, but that my father had mismanaged his inheritance and then taken off with what was left of it without a look back? Or that my mother was a drunk who was more interested in partying than in making sure I had food to eat, let alone Christmas presents or another warm body to celebrate holidays with? I couldn't have it become common knowledge that that's what my family had come to."

"But you were known far and wide as the rich kid at Saunders. How did you keep up appearances that well?" Ella asked, trying to absorb what he was saying.

"I was known as the rich kid at my high school before that, too," he said wryly. "It was mainly the name. I was the kid from the rich family. It takes a lot for impressions to change. Besides, I worked as hard at keeping up that appearance as my mother did to keep up hers—which she did until the day she died in a jet-skiing accident on the French Riviera the first year I was in residency. It may sound strange to you, but my pride was at stake and to protect it and my family's name, I would have done anything. In some ways, I *did* do anything."

"You did?" Ella said, unclear as to what he might be alluding to.

"Here's how it was—the only way I could maintain the illusion was to keep everyone at bay. I couldn't invite friends over—if I did they would see how I was really living or ask too many questions about why my parents weren't ever around. So I could only associate with people at school. Certainly no one could know I was working nights stacking jars of peanut butter and counting myself lucky if the seal was broken on one so I could take it home at no charge.

"But what happens when you feel as if you have as much at risk as I did, is that people become the enemy. People and the possibility of them finding out what you're hiding, of exposing it. They become a threat. And once, when I believed that threat was real…I… Well, I did something pretty rotten."

Ella could only imagine the sad and lonely young man Jacob had been, using arrogance and what was interpreted as snobbishness to keep private what he couldn't bear to become public. And her heart went out to him.

"We can all be driven to do rotten things under dire circumstances," she said compassionately, knowing she was the last person who could cast stones.

"But not all of us do things that could ruin someone else's future. Their life."

Jacob was strangling his tea glass with both hands and staring at it from beneath a dark frown, as if he were lost in his own thoughts, his own past.

Ella wasn't sure he was going to explain that last comment, but she also wasn't sure she should pry. So she let silence reign a moment, waiting to see if he changed the subject or let her in on what she could tell was something that touched a deeper pain than all of his family's neglect and the sorrows of his adolescence put together.

Then, as if he felt the need to confess the whole thing, he said, "Did you know a guy named Smith Parker at Saunders?"

Ella thought for a moment. "No, I didn't."

"Well, he was a student there. For a while, anyway.

We weren't friends, but we had a couple of classes together and knew each other by sight. Sometimes when money was really bad, I'd take whatever I could salvage from the house and sell it at the pawnshop in town to raise cash. I always went on the sly, late at night when I was least likely to be spotted by anyone who knew me. But one night Smith Parker caught me in the act. I went into a panic, figuring that just that was enough to give everything away and—"

"That was when you did something rotten," Ella said, concerned with what that might be.

"I implicated him in a burglary that had happened at one of the sorority houses," Jacob confessed, his voice full of self-loathing. "He hadn't done it—in fact I just met up with him again a few weeks ago and he said he'd figured *I'd* broken into the place and that I was at the pawnshop selling what I'd stolen—which, of course, wasn't the case, either. But right after I told the university's administration just enough to make it look bad for Parker, he left school. As a student, anyway. He never got his degree and ended up working on the maintenance crew at Saunders."

"Because of what you'd told the administration about him?" Ella asked, careful to keep her tone neutral.

"When we accidentally came face-to-face a few weeks ago I decided it was time to make amends. I persuaded him to have a drink with me and apologized, told him I've always carried a load of guilt for what I did to him, for ruining his life. He said he'd quit school of his own volition, but I don't know if that's true."

"It doesn't seem as though it gave you a sense of absolution," Ella observed.

"Like I said, what I did was a rotten thing to do. And even if Parker quit rather than get kicked out because of what I said about him, I have to think that some part of his decision to throw in the towel on his education was my fault."

Ella understood the desperation that had driven him and despite the consequences of his actions, she couldn't condemn him as much as he condemned himself. She also knew there wasn't anything she could say that would change either what he'd done or how he felt about it, so she didn't try. She did, however, decide to get them back to the subject that had started him down this road—the subject of Gilbert Harrison.

"Was Professor Harrison involved in this somehow? Did he do something during that period that became the debt you said you owed? The debt that finally made you decide to help him?"

Jacob shook his head, still staring at his hands around his glass. "No, it was just a whole time in my life that I didn't want to revisit. But Gilbert actually did me two favors, and so I knew I had to go back and help him out even though it stirred old issues for me."

"Two favors?" Ella repeated to urge him on.

"He found me out, too, but not from my going to the pawnshop. Gilbert accidentally discovered that I worked nights at the store. He called me into his office the next day, talked to me about it. He had all my grades in front of him, told me they'd be better if I was concentrating all my energy on my classes. I'm not sure why I did it, but I was honest about what was going on with me. I guess by then I was old enough to be safe from Social Services putting me into the system and charging my parents with abandonment and neglect, so it didn't matter. But it was a big deal to me to tell anyone. Gilbert agreed to keep my secret—that was the first favor he did."

"And the second?"

"The second favor I only suspected he'd had a hand in when it happened. Right after my meeting with Gilbert I was awarded a full scholarship that even paid me a living stipend so I could quit work and just go to college. It seemed to come out of nowhere because I hadn't applied for anything. The benefactor was anonymous but I thought maybe Gilbert had submitted my name. I hounded him until he admitted that he had. Since I didn't have to work, my grades went up and I was able to get into medical school. The scholarships kept coming, all the way through graduation from Harvard, thanks to Gilbert and this benefactor."

"But you still don't know who the benefactor was?" Ella asked carefully.

"I asked Gilbert but he wouldn't even tell me now, after the fact. He said the same way he kept my secret, he kept the secret of the benefactor's identity because that was how the benefactor wanted it." Jacob was quiet for a minute. "Whoever he or she is, they changed my life."

Ella nodded, feeling strongly as if the ball was suddenly in her court. Even though Jacob had no way of knowing that.

But what he'd just told her touched on what she'd been agonizing over since finding out Gilbert Harrison was in trouble. And now it was Ella's turn to look away from him as she considered what to do.

But in her considerations something her sister had said to her that morning came back to her. Sara had asked her how she would feel if she didn't tell what she knew and something bad came of it because she didn't.

"What if Professor Harrison loses his fight with the board?" she asked then, knowing the question was coming out of the blue, but needing an answer to make her own decision.

She felt rather than saw Jacob finally look at her again. "He loses his job."

"I know, but has he made provisions for that possibility? Has he said that if the worst happens, he'll make the best of it? That he'll take early retirement and travel the world? Or do things that maybe he's always thought about doing and never gotten around to? Anything like that?"

She was looking for any indication that she should go on keeping to herself what she'd sworn she would.

When she glanced at Jacob again she found him shaking his head. "Gilbert isn't the man he used to be. His job is his whole life now. It's all he has, especially since his wife died not long ago. I don't even want to think about what he'll do if he loses this fight. I know he can't so much as comprehend where he might go from here if he does. We just have to make sure he wins and keeps his job."

Which was the indication Ella thought she needed. If this was that important to her old professor and he refused to help himself, she was going to have to break her promise so she could do it for him. Even though it meant being as candid with Jacob as he'd just been with her.

This time it was Ella who took a deep breath and sighed it out. Then she began to fiddle with her used napkin, folding it into a star as she said very softly, "I know something. Something that should probably be used in Professor Harrison's defense."

"You do?"

It wasn't easy for Ella to look Jacob in the eye, so she switched her position, sitting with her weight on one hip, her side to the sofa front where she could turn enough to pet the sleeping puppy and aim her focus in that direction rather than directly at Jacob.

"Once upon a time I did something rotten, too," she said, her own regret for that echoing in her voice.

"What could you have done that was rotten?" he asked as if he didn't believe it was possible.

"My senior year at Saunders was a struggle. My parents were both killed in an accident two months into the second semester and my brain just wasn't firing on all burners. My grades plummeted, and I actually pulled an F in my most important political science class—an F that was going to mean I wouldn't be able to graduate. Or ever have any chance of going to law school. I was desperate," she said, sounding it and hoping Jacob could identify with the mirror image of what she'd seen in him. "Not only that, I was also in the throes of grief and not completely myself. And one day I sneaked into the confidential student files to change my grade."

Ella had to pause there to swallow back her own shame. "I've never told a single soul about this before," she whispered.

"It's okay," Jacob assured in a quiet, soothing voice. "Like you said, under dire circumstances, we all do things we wish we hadn't."

Ella nodded but she didn't feel any better. Despite the fact that she appreciated his understanding.

"I got caught," she continued. "After I'd changed the grade but while I still had my nose in files I shouldn't have been in. I was brought before the academic council for my 'suspicious actions.' No one realized the grade had been changed and my professor had gone on a medical leave, so he wasn't around to see what I had done and reveal it. But still, I was where I wasn't supposed to be, nosing into files I shouldn't have been, and it was enough to bring my ethics into question."

"Which would also have kept you out of law school."

"Most likely. But just when I was sure I was going to be thrown out of Saunders anyway, Professor Harrison—who was my adviser—came to my rescue. He told the council that I was working for him, that he'd asked me to file some things and that that was why I was looking at those files. He saved me. I wouldn't be where I am today without him."

From the corner of her eye Ella saw Jacob nod. "The trouble is, I'm afraid if the board heard that story it would only work against Gilbert now. It would support their claim that he crosses the line for his students."

"I agree. But that isn't where I'm going with this. I'm going somewhere much bigger. Much more important…"

Chapter Eight

Ella was having difficulty going through with her decision to reveal the secret she had been keeping about her former professor and advisor at Saunders. But she'd arrived at the point where she was sitting with Jacob, where she'd let him know she had been keeping the secret all these years, and that the secret—if she told it—might be crucial to the professor's defense.

So now that she'd come this far, she felt she had to go on.

"What I need to tell you to help Professor Harrison is about something I discovered when I was going through those files, looking for mine."

"Okay," Jacob said, his tone inviting her to go on.

Ella took another deep breath, resigning herself to breaking her promise, now that she'd begun. "What I discovered in those files were some copies of records about directing scholarships and other monetary gifts to students in need for one reason or another. Notes about where those students believed the money was coming from to conceal the true source." She forced herself to look at Jacob again. "I didn't see your name specifically, but since what I found was enough to prove that Gilbert Harrison was the anonymous benefactor to a whole lot of other people, I'm assuming he was yours, too."

She saw the shock come over Jacob's handsome face.

"Gilbert?"

"After he helped me out of my own mess I thanked him and asked why he'd done it. He said he knew me, knew I was worthy of the help. But he also wanted to know everything I'd seen in the files. I was honest with him, I told him I knew about his private assistance program. He was honest with me, too. He told me that he'd inherited a large sum of money from his grandfather, money his grandfather had won just before he'd passed away.

"Professor Harrison had used some of the money to pay for his own schooling and to help make ends meet for his wife and him so he could stay in the low-paying world of academia, but the rest he decided to use to carry on his grandfather's generosity, to help other people. Since his grandfather had left the money to Gilbert alone—because his grandfather knew that Gilbert was the only family member who would use the money wisely and not squander it recklessly—his grandfather had made him promise not to let anyone know about it."

Ella paused again, allowing Jacob a moment for all she was telling him to sink in.

Then she said, "Professor Harrison insisted that, as repayment for giving me an alibi for being in those files, I swear to two things—that I never again do anything like what I'd done in changing my grade, and that I never breathe a word of what I'd learned about the good deeds he was doing. And until this minute I've kept my word on both counts."

"But now?"

"This man has selflessly helped a lot of students. More than by just listening to them, being a friend to them, giving them a place to sit and talk. He *saved* me—I don't know whether or not you really did do damage to this Smith Parker's life, but *my* whole life, *my* whole future would have been destroyed had I been expelled from Saunders. Would you be a doctor if not for that scholarship money and the stipend that let you quit working nights?"

"No," Jacob answered without having to think about it. "My grades before that wouldn't have gotten me into any medical school, let alone Harvard."

"And we're just two of who knows how many people Professor Harrison helped. Of course, the board doesn't need to hear that he gave me an alibi he probably shouldn't have given me, but it seems to me that they should know the good he's done."

"Even if he doesn't want it known? I mean, I'm glad you told me, but now I'm not sure what to do with the information."

"I've been wrestling with that since last night when

you filled me in on what's happening. But this is a very big thing he's done for a lot of students and it seems to me that if it comes down to a choice of losing the job you said yourself he can't stand losing, or defending him and helping him keep that job by using the good he's done and, by rights, deserves credit for, then it seems to me that I should be the one—or maybe you should be the one—to do for Professor Harrison what he won't do for himself."

Jacob didn't respond to that. And his expression made it obvious that he was now in the dilemma she'd been in since the night before.

"You're in the thick of this with him," she said then. "I'll leave it up to you whether to use what I've told you or not."

"I guess I'll have to think about it."

They'd talked for a long time and it had gotten very late. Ella decided she should probably leave him to his thinking.

"I'd better get home," she said then, kneeling beside the coffee table to begin gathering the debris from their picnic supper.

"You don't have to do that. The cleaning crew comes in overnight and they'll take care of everything," Jacob advised.

"You're sure?"

"Positive. I eat more late-night meals here than I want to admit to, so they know what to do with whatever they come across. I pay extra for it."

Another element was added to the image Ella had had of him as the lonely child earlier—only now the image was of him as a lonely adult who ate dinner alone in his office instead of in a lovely mansion.

Then it occurred to her that for tonight's late-night meal he hadn't been alone, that she was with him, and that if that was the case tonight, it could well be the case on many occasions. That maybe the whole picnic supper was something he did often. With other women...

But even as she suffered a silent wave of jealousy at that thought, Ella didn't really believe it. Not when she remembered how inept he'd been at inviting her in the first place.

And remembering that, learning that he frequently ate in his office, went a long way in making her feel special all over again at the idea that he'd planned this for her and included her in something he did on a less romantic scale at other times. It went a long way in making her feel more special than it was safe for her to feel, given that she knew she was supposed to be keeping her guard up.

They both stood.

"Did you get your car back?" Jacob asked as they did.

Ella wondered if she was right in hearing a note of hopefulness in his tone, if he might be hoping for the opportunity to take her home again tonight. Which, at that moment, would have pleased her, too.

But it wasn't to be.

"The mechanic finished with the repairs this afternoon," she answered.

"Oh," he said, a bit awkwardly. "I'll walk you down to the parking lot, then."

He didn't make a move to get Champ or to do anything else that might have let her believe he was leaving work for the day, so she said, "You and Champ aren't going home?"

Jacob nodded toward his desk. "I still have some case files to update yet."

Ella nodded, getting her purse from beside the sofa and putting the strap over her shoulder as Jacob motioned for her to lead the way out of the office.

"Will Champ be okay up here by herself?" she said when Jacob didn't move to take the sleeping puppy with him.

"She's down for the count. She'll never even know I'm gone."

He did close his inner-office door after them, though, and then the door that led to the corridor and the elevator.

A member of the building security team happened to be in the elevator when it came. The man greeted Jacob and they exchanged small talk on the ride to the first floor where Ella and Jacob went out to the parking lot.

It was nearly empty when they got there, and as they crossed to Ella's sedan Jacob said, "After your acupuncture tomorrow night we'll go to the meeting with Gilbert's old students. Would you like to grab a bite to eat after that?"

"Okay," Ella agreed as she pushed the button on her key chain to unlock her car door as they drew near.

Jacob made sure to reach the sedan ahead of her to open the door, standing on the outside of it and holding it for her with his hands on the upper rim of the raised window.

Ella stepped to the inside of the door but stayed there, not getting behind the wheel so she could be eye to eye with him to say good-night.

"Thanks for dinner…and everything…tonight," she said, referring only obliquely to the fact that he'd so nonjudgmentally listened to the tale of her sordid past.

But apparently the reference was too oblique because he looked confused and said, "Everything?"

"Being as open as you were with me and not raising an eyebrow at my own misdeeds. I've been holding them in for a long time, and it kind of felt good to let it out for the first time."

He nodded as if he understood that, too. "Those things get heavy when you're carrying them alone. Believe me, I know. But I do think that even if I decide to tell the group about Gilbert being the benefactor, they don't need to know the details of *how* you found out any more than the board does. All anyone needs to hear is that you *did* find out—in case you were worrying about tomorrow night."

In that moment she was surprised to realize that she'd trusted him and how much. "I appreciate that," she said.

He seemed more engrossed in looking at her then, than in thinking more about Gilbert Harrison or his problems. He took another deep breath and sighed, almost as if he were reluctantly conceding something. "I really like…being with you."

Had he been going to say he really liked her? Had he just chickened out at the end?

That possibility made Ella smile. "I really like talking to you, too," she said with an edge of amusement to her voice.

He seemed to know how she'd interpreted his comment, but his widening grin said he didn't mind. That she might be right in assuming it was she he liked.

And then he leaned forward, over the car door, and kissed her.

There was something about this kiss, though—unlike the quickie kiss of the previous evening—that seemed to have some consideration behind it. It wasn't impulsive. It had the feel of a kiss he'd thought about before he'd done it. A kiss that he might have thought a *lot* about.

This kiss was slower, more studied. This kiss gave her time to react. To respond. It gave them both the chance to move past the initial meeting of mouth to mouth and learn the feel of supple lips that parted only slightly, that grew comfortable with each other, that relaxed and simply enjoyed the sensations.

This kiss lasted long enough for Ella to feel Jacob's breath against her skin. Long enough for her to wish the car door wasn't separating them. Long enough to wish to have his arms around her, his hands on her back or in her hair. Long enough to wish for their bodies to be up close together…

But none of that happened before they finally parted. A lazy, natural parting that Ella regretted nonetheless.

Then Jacob took a step backward, away from the car, and gave her another smile that wasn't at all like any she'd seen from him up to that moment. A smile that really seemed to come from the heart, warm and almost intimate, leaving her with no question that it was for her and for her alone.

"I'll see you tomorrow night," he said in a tone that told her he was looking forward to it. Looking forward to seeing her again. To being with her.

Ella nodded, unsure if her own voice would be strong enough to carry when that kiss still had her temperature on the rise and everything else inside her was weak and willowy.

Jacob turned on his heel and left her then, giving her a view of him from behind that she knew she'd be taking to bed with her tonight.

That and the memory of a sweet, sexy little kiss from a man she was coming to suspect had a soft center hidden deep inside.

Chapter Nine

"I have something to tell you all…"

Ella sat in a circle of folding chairs in an empty storefront next door to a small grocery store called Westport's Emporium. It was owned and operated by David and Sandra Westport, both of whom had gone to Saunders University and were working on Gilbert Harrison's behalf along with Jacob.

The Westports had arranged to have Thursday evening's meeting in the vacant shop beside their own. Ella had been introduced to the married couple, as well as to Kathryn Price—whose beautiful face Ella recognized from magazine covers during her days as a model. She was sitting beside Nate Williams whom, as Ella had told Jacob, she knew professionally. After exchanging amenities with everyone, Jacob had taken the lead with the group.

"Ella has told me something about Gilbert that I think is pretty important, and after considering what to do with the information, I've decided to throw it out to everyone so we can work with it, not work with it, whatever…"

On the drive to the meeting Jacob had let Ella know that he'd come to the decision he'd just announced. He'd asked if she would like to be the one to tell the group that she knew for a fact that Gilbert was the mystery benefactor to so many of Saunders's students in need. She'd thought it would be better coming from him, especially since once the information was relayed it was up to Jacob and the rest of the group to discuss how to proceed from there. Ella didn't want to infringe on the core group that Professor Harrison himself had banded together to help him.

While Jacob spoke, Ella was peripherally aware of the other people sitting in the circle listening to him. From the small talk that had preceded the meeting, Ella had gathered that this joint effort had brought Nate Williams and Kathryn Price together in more than a common-cause sort of way. Apparently, they'd become a couple themselves and now sat holding hands.

It was slightly odd to see Nate Williams showing affection and obviously deep feelings for Kathryn. Or for anyone, for that matter. Knowing him only professionally—in terms of his defense of several shady characters who Ella had prosecuted—Ella had always thought of him as a shark. But here he was, clearly smitten with

Kathryn. And on top of that, he was also donating his time and energy to take depositions from members of the group to aid Gilbert Harrison's case—something Ella had only learned this evening when Jacob had told her he'd spent his lunchtime with Nate, giving his formal statement in favor of Professor Harrison.

It was a different side of the man that Ella found interesting.

Not as interesting as she found Jacob, however.

He'd been leaving his office just as Dr. Schwartz called Ella in for her acupuncture, telling them that he was going home to deposit Champ for the evening. He'd returned just in time to say good-night to Kim Schwartz and usher Ella out of the office and down to his Porsche.

But putting Champ in her crate was not the only thing he'd done while he'd been gone. He'd come back freshly showered, shaved, smelling wonderful and wearing a pair of navy blue slacks and a pale blue sport shirt. Both blues worked together to accentuate the even darker hue of his eyes, and Ella couldn't help wondering if, somewhere over the years, someone had told him that.

But whether he was aware of it or not, she could hardly tear her own gaze away from the sight he presented, sitting there with his broad shoulders dwarfing the back of the folding chair, one ankle resting atop the opposite knee, and a big, thick-fingered hand riding the muscular thigh of that upturned leg as his deep, commanding voice filled the space in conclusion of what he'd just told everyone.

"Well, of course we have to use this to help Gilbert. Right away. Tomorrow. Today. Yesterday!" Kathryn Price said the moment Jacob finished.

The former model's enthusiasm drew Ella from her study—and admiration—of Jacob. Followed by rapidly increasing support of Kathryn's sentiments from the Westports and Nate Williams, Ella felt the need to put the brakes on, to slow things down.

"I don't know about that," she said slowly, finally speaking up.

"You don't?" Jacob said, surprise tingeing his tone.

"Maybe this is coming from my own guilt over having told something I promised I wouldn't tell, but I don't think anything should be rushed into. Remember that Professor Harrison has gone to great lengths to hide the fact that he's been a generous benefactor for so many years to so many people. That even now—when it could help him—he hasn't told anyone. I think that we—or you—need to tread carefully. I was hoping you would move from here to possibly just making him aware that you've found this out and using your influence on him to persuade him to give his permission."

"The voice of reason," Jacob said, smiling at her. Then, to the rest of the group, he said, "I think Ella's right. We can't just charge the gates with something Gilbert has been trying to keep quiet about. He should decide whether to use it in his defense or not. We can let him know that we know, that we'd like to use it, and see what he says."

"And don't expect him to be happy that it's gotten

out, because he won't be," Ella cautioned, again from her own sense of guilt.

"I just wish we could present it to him in a united front," Kathryn said. "A *completely* united front—with Rachel and even Cassidy on our side—then we'd really have some oomph."

Jacob leaned sideways in his chair until his shoulder touched Ella's, angling his head in her direction and setting off a barrage of glittery, tingling sensations all through her with that barely-there contact.

"Rachel James and Cassidy Maxwell," he explained, filling Ella in. "Cassidy was very fond of Gilbert, and we know she'd want to help him so we were hoping to get her involved. But at some point she moved to London and so far we haven't been able to locate her. And Rachel has been working with us until recently but—"

"Yeah, where *is* Rachel?" Nate Williams demanded, overhearing Jacob's explanation to Ella.

It was Sandra Westport who fielded that question. "I called and left her two messages about the meeting tonight. She didn't call me back but I was really hoping she'd show up."

"She's acting weird," Kathryn pointed out.

"I know," Sandra said. "I'm worried about her."

"Why? Is something wrong with her?" Nate asked.

"She's been really withdrawn—you must have noticed that the last time we were all together." Sandra's tone and expression gave evidence to just how worried she really was.

"I know *I* noticed," David Westport contributed. "How could you miss it? The last time we met to talk about Gilbert, she was distracted. She couldn't even keep up with what we were hashing through. I wasn't sure if she had something else on her mind or if she'd just lost interest in Gilbert's problems."

"I certainly have had the feeling that something's bothering her," Kathryn said.

"David and I were thinking that maybe we should talk to her, find out what's going on," Sandra put in.

"That might be a good idea," Jacob said. "I know I came away from the last time I saw her wondering what was wrong."

"And then there's the Cassidy issue," Nate said, deftly changing the subject.

Besides being familiar with Nate Williams, the name Cassidy Maxwell was one that Ella recognized, and now that the conversation had circled back to where it had begun, she decided to speak up. "I know someone who knew Cassidy Maxwell at Saunders. Maybe there's something I can do to help in that arena. Why hasn't anyone been able to locate her?"

It was Jacob who answered. "All we know is that she's in London—*somewhere* in London. We haven't been able to find out exactly where so we can reach her. Would the person you know have a work or a home address, or a phone number, or even an e-mail address?"

"The person I know is Eric Barnes…anyone familiar with him?"

Heads shook, and two of the group muttered in the negative.

Ella went on. "Eric was at Saunders, too. He graduated the same year I did. We had a few classes together, worked on some of the same campaigns and committees. He was longtime friends with Cassidy Maxwell. In fact, if I'm remembering right, I think I might have met her briefly once through him. I know he talked about her a lot. Actually, I always wondered if he didn't sort of have a crush on her, but they'd grown up together and she was younger and… Well, as far as I know, they were always just close friends. But they *were* close. If anyone knows exactly where she is or how to reach her, I'd think it would be Eric. And even if he doesn't want to give out her address or phone number, maybe he could contact her himself, tell her what's going on with Professor Harrison and have her get back to one of you."

"That'd be great!" Sandra Westport said. "And the sooner the better on this one for sure. We're running out of possibilities—and time."

"I'll call Eric first thing tomorrow."

Then the meeting came to an end so the Westports could get home to kids they'd left with a sitter. Everyone said good-night and filtered out of the empty shop into the evening air.

And Ella could only hope she'd done the right thing, and that her former professor wouldn't hate her for it.

Chapter Ten

"How do you feel about sushi?" Jacob asked Ella when they were in the Porsche again after the meeting.

"I feel like it's *raw fish,*" she said with disdain.

Jacob laughed. "But it's really *good* raw fish. I take it you've never had it?"

"My sister likes it but it doesn't appeal to me."

"The place I'm thinking of has a lot of cooked options, too. They even serve steak and a nice grilled salmon, if you don't want to venture off the beaten path at all. What do you say?"

"Steak or salmon I can do. I make no promises about sushi."

He cast her a pleased grin that set off those glittery, tingling sensations again as he pulled into traffic.

"How fancy is this place?" she asked then, glancing

down at the khaki slacks and bright-red, short-sleeved camp shirt she was wearing, thinking that she again just had her hair caught at her crown in a scrunchee and wasn't dressed for anything that wasn't completely casual.

Jacob took his eyes off the road long enough to smile at her. "You look just right," he assured her with what sounded almost like a bit of innuendo in his voice and delighted her more than it should.

The restaurant was about halfway between the Westports' store and Jacob's office so it didn't take long to get there. Because it was 9:30 and past the dinner rush only a few tables were occupied and they got right in.

The dimly lit, art-deco enclave was quiet, allowing them to talk without raising their voices over any kind of noise.

Jacob convinced Ella to try a shrimp tempura sushi roll along with her salmon, and then gave her a lesson in using the chopsticks that were the only utensils at each place setting.

Ella was completely uncoordinated at it, and by the time their food arrived they were both laughing at her attempts. They laughed even harder when, without being asked, their waiter brought her a fork.

"Oh, great, I've embarrassed myself in public thanks to you," she said after the waiter left.

"Is it my fault you can't even do what little Asian children can?" he countered in fun.

As they ate, Jacob tried to persuade, cajole and tease Ella into tasting the lovely looking variety of rolls and pieces of tuna resting over small mounds of rice, but she held fast to her no-raw-fish stance. She did enjoy the battered and deep-fried shrimp in her own roll, and her salmon was wonderful, too.

When they'd finished the main course and were sharing a square of tiramisu—after more laughing over why a sushi restaurant was serving an Italian dessert—Jacob sat up straighter and slung one arm over the back of his chair, pinning Ella in place with that navy-blue gaze.

"So, this Eric Barnes," he said, "he's someone from Saunders that you keep in touch with?"

"Sort of," Ella answered. Was she hearing things or was there a note of something that sounded like jealousy in his tone?

"Sort of?"

"It isn't as if it's a regular appointment or that we're actually what you would consider friends. It's more like we're friendly acquaintances who went to college together and have now become people who seem to run into each other repeatedly. We operate in the same circles, to some extent, I guess you could say. Our offices are only blocks apart, and we happen to meet at social events now and then. He's a political advisor and we've worked with some of the same candidates during elections—things like that."

"But you have his phone number and feel free to call him?"

If it wasn't jealousy in Jacob's voice, Ella didn't know what it was. And she couldn't suppress a secret smile over it.

"Well, we do go way back. But our relationship is

pretty much the same now as it was when we were in college. We've had lunch and dinner together on occasion, we've shared a few pizzas over envelope stuffing. There's been a time or two when one or the other of us has needed a favor of some kind and we've called. That's what I'll do tomorrow."

"So you've *never* dated or anything?"

Ella didn't think there was any mistaking it by then—Jacob Weber was jealous at the thought that she might have some kind of romantic relationship with Eric Barnes. And it tickled her pink. Even though it shouldn't have mattered at all.

"Well, there was that torrid affair we had in college and the pact we made to meet at the same time each year at a hideaway in the Berkshires for mad, passionate, nonstop lovemaking. But other than that…" Ella said with a straight face.

This time it was Jacob who smiled, a bit chagrined as he realized what she suspected of him.

Still, he played along. "What time of the year?"

"Spring," she answered without skipping a beat. "When love is in bloom."

"And if either of you are involved with other people?"

"We lie to them and leave our real lives behind," Ella said very theatrically.

"Good to know," Jacob responded with a single arched eyebrow.

Ella laughed at him and returned to the question he'd asked before she'd made up this story. "I've never dated Eric Barnes. Like I said at the meeting, I always thought he had a soft spot for his friend Cassidy Maxwell. Maybe they finally got together, it ended badly, and that's why she's incognito in London."

"I'm sure she's not incognito, it's just that no one was willing to fly to England and walk the streets calling her name in hopes that she'd happen to hear. But I *hope* this Eric Barnes didn't get together with her and have it end badly—he'd be less likely to help us out if that's the case."

Ella made a seductress's face and batted her eyelashes. "Leave it to me. Eric never could resist my charms."

"No doubt," Jacob said with another grin.

The restaurant was obviously closing so he paid the bill and they left.

As Jacob opened the passenger door for Ella, he said, "So what did you think about this place? I know the raw fish is great, how was the cooked?"

"Really, really good, too. I'll have to tell my sister to try it. Her husband isn't crazy about the raw stuff, either, so they could both have what they like—the way we did," Ella answered as he set the Porsche in motion to travel the rest of the distance to his office.

"Your sister, Sara, who went to Saunders with me? Or do you have more than one sister?"

"Just the one."

"Do you have any brothers?"

"No, there's just Sara and me."

"And Sara is married?"

"She is. To a great guy named Andy."

"And they've produced the daughter who has toys at your apartment," Jacob concluded.

"Right. Janey. She's turning three years old tomorrow, as a matter of fact."

"It sounds as if you all like each other."

Ella laughed. "We do. I know a lot of families don't get along, but Sara and I have always been best friends as well as sisters—as hokey as that might sound. We couldn't be any closer."

"And since you describe her husband as a great guy, I take it you're close to him, too?"

"We all grew up together, actually, so I was friends with Andy before he was my brother-in-law."

"The boy-next-door married the girl-next-door?"

"The boy-across-the-street married the girl-across-the-street," she corrected. "Sara and Andy were childhood sweethearts. Which means that Andy was around our house so much, for so long, that he's always just seemed like a brother to me."

"But not to your sister?"

"Apparently not," Ella answered with another laugh.

"And where did this family bonding take place?"

Ella glanced over at Jacob, knowing that the note of skepticism in his voice came from the fact that he'd spent such a solitary life growing up, a life so devoid of close relationships of any kind that it wasn't easy for him to understand the sort of life she'd had as a kid. So she didn't take offense at that hint of the more sardonic Jacob Weber peeking through.

"Sara, Andy and Janey live in Boston the same as I do now, but back then we all lived outside of the city, a few miles from Saunders. That's why both Sara and I went there—so we could live at home and not have the expense of dormitories or apartments along with tuition and books. Well, that and that we liked it at home."

"You were both close to your parents before their deaths, too?" He said this as if it seemed almost unfathomable to him.

"We were all very, very close. We loved our parents. They were warm and fun and they doted on us like mad. They weren't rich, but we were spoiled as rotten as their budget would allow."

"It must have been nice," he mused.

Ella almost felt guilty for having been as honest with him about this as she had been. She hadn't intended to rub his nose in the fact that she had had a good home life while his had been so abysmal. But now that she *had* been honest about it, she couldn't take it back and didn't exactly know what to say.

"What does great-guy-Andy do for a living?" Jacob asked then.

That seemed like a safe subject so Ella seized it. "He's a whiz with computers in about every way you can name, but he makes his living writing software. I know that makes him sound dull, but he's not. He's a lot of fun."

And then, without thinking about it before she took the leap, Ella said, "Tomorrow night is Janey's birthday party. Would you like to come and meet everyone?"

The words were barely out of her mouth when a dozen things raced through her mind. A dozen reasons why she never should have said it at all. There was the asking-him-to-meet-her-family issue. There was the asking-him-on-an-unbusiness-related-date issue. There was the rubbing-his-nose-in-her-close-family issue. There was the Sara-hated-Jacob-Weber issue. And there were so many stepping-out-of-bounds issues she just couldn't count them.

Yet even given all that, she was still disappointed when that invitation was enough to bring their conversation to a screeching halt.

Making matters worse, not only did Jacob not reject the idea, he didn't even address it.

Instead he said, "Here we are," as if she hadn't extended the invitation at all.

Despite the fact that Ella could see for herself that they'd just pulled into his office parking lot, into the space right beside her car, she glanced beyond the Porsche's interior as if this was news to her.

Jacob turned off the engine, removed the key from the ignition and only then did he acknowledge anything to do with her reference to the next night.

"That's right, tomorrow is Friday and there's no acupuncture, is there?"

Not an answer but an evasion.

But Ella thought that maybe that was for the best, so she went along with it. "No, no acupuncture. I'll be doing acupressure and meditation for the next three days."

He nodded. "It'll be good for your body to have a rest," he said, opening his door and getting out of the car.

Ella did the same thing before he could reach her

side and open the passenger door for her, meeting him face-to-face there between her sedan and his Porsche.

"Thanks for dinner and letting me tag along to your meeting tonight," she said as she pushed the button on her key ring to unlock her own door. "I'll call Eric Barnes as soon as I can in the morning and let you know what he has to say."

"Good," Jacob said, sounding as if he wasn't really listening. His eyes were on her intently from where he was standing with his back to her car, effectively blocking her from getting in. But his expression was unreadable even though they were directly under a pole light that provided plenty of illumination.

"I'm just glad there's something I can do," Ella added, trying to stick to the impersonal.

"If you can connect us with Cassidy Maxwell that'll be a big accomplishment," he said, continuing to watch her and to sound distracted.

Neither of them said anything for a moment and so Ella finally opted for taking the initiative.

"I should probably go," she said then, aiming her gaze behind him at her car and wanting to dive into it to escape the sudden awkwardness she'd caused by that invitation.

"Probably," he agreed. But he didn't move. He just stayed where he was, looking at her with those piercing blue eyes.

"And you should probably get home to Champ," Ella reminded.

"Probably."

Jacob took a step forward, and Ella thought he was freeing the path to her door.

He wasn't, though.

He was coming to stand closer in front of her.

To reach both of his hands to her arms, running them up and down in a gentle massage that slid under the sleeves of her shirt in a way that seemed somehow very intimate and helped immensely in breaking up some of that awkwardness she was experiencing.

"I'm beginning to feel like a teenager—always saying goodbye to you in the school parking lot," he said.

"So our parents don't find out about us and forbid us to ever see each other again," Ella added, joking to lighten the tone.

"I'd hate to never see you again," he said.

Ella couldn't be sure if he was kidding to play along or if he was serious. It sounded as if he were serious but he was smiling a small, secret smile that made her wonder.

Then, under his breath and more to himself than to her, he said, "I'd *really* hate it."

He pulled her toward him and when Ella raised her chin to continue to look up at him, his mouth met hers.

And regardless of the fact that he might have had reservations about going to her niece's birthday party, he clearly had none when it came to kissing her.

No more than Ella had about kissing him back. Because the instant his lips touched hers, it completely wiped away any remnants of the awkwardness left by that unanswered invitation and left her awash in thoughts only of him. Of how good it was to have those big, capable hands caressing her arms. Of how good it was to feel the heat of his body so near. Of how good *he* was at kissing…

He parted his lips and coaxed hers to part, too, and it occurred to Ella that it hadn't taken long for this to become familiar, for her to know the signs and be able to follow them, for this to be something she didn't think she could get enough of.

She laid her hands on his chest, feeling the hard wall of muscle behind his smooth, crisp shirt, relishing having it beneath her palms. She breathed in the scent of cologne he must have applied when he'd gone home with Champ, and could smell faint hints of the fresh ginger he'd eaten and enjoyed the bit of spice it added.

Jacob wrapped his arms around her and brought her up against him, making her aware of her own body and its response to his kiss, to him. Her breasts seemed to be straining against her bra, reaching out to him with taut tips that sent little shards of joy all through her when they met his body. Little shards of joy she wanted more of, so she slipped her own arms around his sides, flattening her front to his and getting to feel the broad, hard expanse of his back for the first time.

His lips parted still more and so did hers. It didn't surprise her when his tongue introduced itself. First just to the scant inner edge of her lower lip and then her upper.

She opened her mouth wider, welcoming him, willing—eager—to deepen this kiss, to take this one step farther, as her body was coming awake and urging more still.

He took the advantage she'd given, widening his own mouth, sending his tongue to explore, to greet hers, cradling her head when he pressed it back to accommodate that kiss.

Ella met and matched his tongue, learning the texture, the circle dance he wanted to lead, following and adding a few twists of her own, frolicking in the game, the challenge, the pleasure of it while more of those glittery, tingling sensations began to twitter all through her.

But with those glittery, tingling sensations came other things. Things that made her want more than that hot kiss in the parking lot. Things that made her want to shed clothes. To feel his skin against her skin. To feel his hands, his mouth, on her breasts. To feel his body and hers together…

But they *were* in the parking lot. And none of that was going to happen. Not there. Not then. None of it *could* happen with this man she barely knew. This man who hadn't even made up a polite excuse to turn down her offer to bring him to Janey's birthday party.

So, as much as Ella was enjoying that kiss, she began to take steps to end it.

She eased back ever so little.

She withdrew her arms from around him and insinuated her hands between them again.

Then she drew her mouth from his.

"At my high school we had rent-a-cops who patrolled the parking lot and were likely to hose down two people doing this," she said with a forced laugh.

Jacob didn't seem to take offense at her ending their kiss because his response was a raspy-sounding chuckle before he dropped his forehead to hers and conceded,

"I've never been caught at it here, but it doesn't seem beyond the realm of possibility given the heat we were generating."

"It was getting a little warm," Ella agreed.

"And we don't want to be hosed down."

"I know I don't."

"So we stop," he concluded.

And they didn't start again—even though that was what Ella wanted enough to entertain thoughts of it. Thoughts of even moving this across the street to his town house.

For a while they remained the way they were, though—his arms loosely around her now, her hands flat against his chest, his head lowered to the top of hers.

And then, out of the blue, he said, "You know, I'm racking my brain, but unless I went to one when I was three and just don't remember it, I don't think I've ever been to a birthday party for a three-year-old."

"No?" Ella said, unsure why he'd brought this up again when he'd avoided talking about it before. Unsure, too, what he was getting at.

He stood straighter then, and Ella looked up at him, seeing a soft smile playing about the corners of that mouth that she just wanted more of.

"Are they fun?" he asked with an arched eyebrow that made him too appealing.

"Birthday parties for three-year-olds?" she repeated to get her own wandering mind on track. "They're fun for three-year-olds," she said, proceeding cautiously on territory that had already proved treacherous.

"But not for the adults. And you just asked me because you wanted me to be miserable?" he inquired.

"It isn't *miserable* for the adults. It's entertaining to watch the kids, and Sara will serve an amazing buffet dinner for the adults that will make it worthwhile. There are worse times to be had," Ella said, not wanting to oversell it.

"And I'd be there with you."

Okay, so that was enough to send little goose bumps up her arms. But she tried to ignore them.

"You would be," she confirmed.

"In that case, I think I'd like to go."

Had he just needed time to ponder it?

That seemed possible. And the fact that this was the decision—made on what appeared to be solely a desire to be with her—pleased Ella enough to allow him absolution for the delay. And for the less-than-good feelings it had produced.

She must not have accepted his acceptance of her invitation quick enough, however, because then he said, "Is that okay? Do you still want me to go?"

"I do," she confirmed without hesitation this time. "If you're sure you *want* to go."

"I'm sure."

He dipped his head down to kiss her again—only a chaste kiss—before he let go of her.

"And how about if I pick you up at your door so we can bypass this parking lot for once?" he said then.

"I'd like that."

"I'll get your address from your file. What time?"

"If you pick me up at six-thirty we should get there when we're supposed to."

"I'll see you then, then," he said, smiling at his own repetition.

He turned and opened her car door, waiting until she was behind the wheel to close it again.

"Tomorrow night, six-thirty," he said, as if she needed reminding, before he tapped the top of her car, gave her a small wave and got out of the way so she could leave.

Ella started her car and put it into gear, waving back as she pulled out of her spot.

And that was when it really sank in that tomorrow night she would be bringing Jacob Weber to her sister's house. Her sister, who vehemently disliked him.

But in the rosy glow left by that kiss the good doctor had just given her, she found it impossible to worry.

Instead, that kiss and the fact that she was going to get to see Jacob again the next night were all that were on her mind the whole way home.

Chapter Eleven

First thing Friday morning Ella put in a call to Eric Barnes. As always, he was friendly, cordial, happy to hear from her. He was also in a rush to get to a meeting and couldn't talk right then. But when Ella told him it was important, he suggested they meet for lunch at a sandwich shop midway between their offices.

Then Ella made the second call she needed to make, feeling far more trepidation about it.

"Don't hate me," she said to her sister when Sara answered the phone on the other end of the line.

"Why would I ever hate you, El?" a confused Sara asked.

"If I had an affair with your husband, you'd hate me," Ella pointed out, leading into what she had to tell her sister with something she thought was far worse than what she was actually going to reveal in hopes that after that, bringing Jacob to Janey's birthday party would seem like peanuts.

It didn't work because Sara merely laughed at the very idea. "You and Andy? An affair? Uh-huh, right."

"I'm just saying, hypothetically, you'd hate me if I had an affair with Andy."

"But anything short of that? Probably I wouldn't hate you."

"Oh, now it's just *probably*."

"Do you know how many things I have to do today?" Sara demanded then, clearly not wanting any more beating around the bush.

"Okay, but promise you won't hate me when I tell you this."

"I won't hate you," Sara said.

"I invited Jacob Weber to the party tonight and he accepted."

"I hate you."

Ella laughed and then cajoled, "Come on..."

"You didn't really do that, right? This is an April Fool's joke in September—you just thought you'd do it early to get me."

"No, I really did do it," Ella confessed.

"Ahh, El..." Sara groaned her complaint. "Are you *trying* to ruin the party?"

"I had dinner with him again last night and he was asking about you all and it just slipped out—did he want to come tonight and meet everyone?"

"And he actually said he *did?*"

Ella judiciously omitted the hesitation that had preceded the acceptance and said, "He did."

"Couldn't you have just had an affair with Andy instead?"

Ella laughed again and repeated, "Come on, Sara…"

"I can't believe His Imperial Highness Jacob Weber said he'd come. He wouldn't even deign to do a class project with the likes of me and my kind, and now he's lowering his standards so much he'll come to my home?"

Back to the poli-sci-class story.

Only now Ella knew why Jacob had pretended he thought he was better than everyone else. Why he wouldn't have wanted to be in a group, why he would have requested to work alone. That detachment had protected his secret. A secret Ella didn't feel at liberty to tell. Not even to Sara.

So instead she said, "He's different now, Sara. He can still be a little rough around the edges, but honestly, that isn't all there is to him. He has a good sense of humor, he's kind and caring and compassionate in his own way, he's—"

"He's sucked you in."

"He hasn't sucked me in. I'd heard the worst about him before I met him—from you and from someone at work—so I expected an ogre. And like I said, he has a few rough edges. But they're protective rough edges and what they protect is something—*someone*—worth getting to know."

"What's going on, El?"

"What do you mean, what's going on? Nothing is going on."

"Something is going on if you're telling me Jacob Weber is someone worth getting to know. Just how well have you gotten to know him?"

The insinuation in her sister's tone was unmistakable.

"I haven't gotten to know him the way you're implying. But I am getting to know him as a person and…well, I like him," Ella admitted reluctantly. But her reluctance wasn't only because she knew her sister wouldn't approve. It was also because Ella knew she shouldn't be fostering her attraction to Jacob. That having another man in her life—now or maybe ever— wasn't in her game plan. That her game plan was to have the child she had her heart set on and that all her energies should be devoted to that and that alone.

"You *like* him?" Sara repeated. "As in *romantically?*"

Visions of that kiss that had ended the previous evening pranced through Ella's mind. That kiss that had kept her awake until late last night replaying itself and replaying itself and replaying itself. Turning her on all over again. Making her wonder what would have happened if she hadn't ended it. Making her wish on some level that she hadn't.

But that wasn't what she told her sister.

"You know I'm not looking for romance," she said emphatically. Emphasizing it to herself as much as to Sara.

"But have you found it, anyway?" Sara asked, sounding loath to even venture the question.

"No," Ella answered, hoping she wasn't lying. "It's just that I've had a good time with Jacob, I enjoy his company, and I'm telling you there's a side of him that you haven't even met that's *worth* meeting. So I invited him to Janey's birthday party and he said he'd come, and it isn't a big deal."

"Seems like it is," Sara said suspiciously.

"It's only a big deal because I know you don't like Jacob. But I want you to meet him again now, so you can see that he isn't what you thought he was."

"Oh, so you're doing this for *me?*"

"I'm doing this just because I wanted to do it. I wanted him to meet Andy and Janey and you—again. And because I wanted you guys to meet him."

"Because you want him?"

"No, not because I *want* him want him," Ella insisted, telling herself that even though she might want to see him, to spend time with him, even though she might want him to kiss her, she didn't want *him*—as in want him in any kind of serious involvement or relationship sort of way.

But her own thoughts were becoming too convoluted, and it was frustrating her, and that frustration finally came out in impatience with her sister. "Don't make this into something it isn't, okay? I've spent some time with this guy, one thing led to another and I asked him to the party tonight—not as any big, dramatic thing, just as a friendly gesture thing—it doesn't mean I *want* him or that he wants me or that there's any kind of romance going on."

Except yet another replay of that kiss in her mind made her feel guilty...

"Okay, okay," Sara conceded. "Jacob Weber is coming to the party tonight. I'll be nice."

Ella laughed a little. "Thank you."

"But honestly, El, *couldn't* you have just had an affair with Andy?" Sara joked again.

"I'll put it on my to-do list if it will make you feel better."

"It might make me feel better than seeing you with Jacob Weber. Be careful with that guy."

"After Brandon I'm careful with *all* guys," Ella insisted.

"I hope so," Sara said.

"You don't have to hope so, you can count on it," Ella said, flashing back much too vividly to sacrifices she'd made to please her former husband. Sacrifices that she was paying a very high price for, that may have cost her what she'd wanted most for as long as she could remember.

But she didn't go into that with her sister. Instead, she said, "Now let me talk to my niece so I can sing her 'Happy Birthday.'"

"I'll get her. And I'll see you tonight," Sara said.

Ella tried not to notice the worried note in her sister's voice. She tried not to worry herself as she waited for her niece to come to the phone.

But there in her mind was still the memory of that kiss.

That hot, hot, hot kiss.

And the heat that lingered from it even now....

"Turkey on whole wheat, veggie sticks instead of chips. BLT on toast, potato salad, two pickles."

The waitress set the turkey sandwich in front of Ella

and the BLT on Eric Barnes's place mat. After making sure neither of them needed anything else, the jowly faced older woman put their check on the end of the table and left them to dine undisturbed in the crowded restaurant.

"I'm glad you called. It's been a while since we've run into each other," Eric Barnes said.

"It has," Ella agreed as they both took bites of their sandwiches.

They'd already gone through the amenities and done a little catching up after putting in their order. And since Eric had let her know from the start that he had another meeting to get to before the lunch hour was up, Ella decided to cut to the chase.

"The reason I wanted to see you has to do with Gilbert Harrison—remember him? From Saunders?" she asked.

"I'd never forget him. English professor, student advisor, baseball coach, friend to all…. He got me a job as a poli-sci TA when I was at Saunders," he answered just before taking a bite of pickle.

"Have you heard what's going on with him?"

Eric was a nice-looking man with dark hair dusted with a touch of premature gray. He had very black eyes, and the brows over them rose in question, letting her know—despite the fact that his mouth was full—that he wasn't aware of anything going on with their former teacher.

"I hadn't heard, either, until this week," Ella said. She filled him in on the details of the professor's problems with the administration.

"That's lousy," was Eric's response when she'd finished. "It's also a low blow to someone who didn't earn it."

"I agree. Which is why I asked if there was anything I could do to help, and that's what led me to you today," Ella summed up, neatly getting to her purpose for this lunch.

"There's something I can do?"

Eric had always been a quick study. It wasn't any wonder that he was as successful as he was.

"Professor Harrison has asked for help from a core group of his past students. People he chose for reasons I'm not privy to. But that group wants to enlist the help of Cassidy Maxwell—they know she was very fond of the professor and they're sure she'd want to help—but no one has a clue as to how to get hold of her. I remembered that you were close to her when we were in college, and I thought you might be able to lend a hand in that area."

Ella watched Eric's expression cloud. "I haven't seen or talked to or heard from Cassidy in…in a really long time. Since before her graduation from Saunders, as a matter of fact."

"Apparently she's somewhere in London—that's as much information as anyone has on her," Ella said, studying Eric's reaction and wondering suddenly if she might be venturing into tender territory when it came to his feelings for Cassidy.

"I know she's in London," Eric said. "She's assistant to the ambassador there."

"So you've kept tabs on her even though the two of you lost touch?" Ella asked.

"I wouldn't say I've kept tabs on her, no," Eric was quick to contradict. So quick it seemed defensive. "But political circles are smaller than you might think. Word gets around."

He seemed uncomfortable with the subject. And certainly not eager to jump in on Gilbert Harrison's—or anyone else's—behalf when it came to Cassidy Maxwell.

But Ella felt strongly about helping their old teacher, and she'd promised to do what she could to find a way to get in touch with Eric's friend, so she wasn't going to give in.

"Could we try to reach her through the ambassador's office?"

Eric must have lost his appetite because he pushed the second half of his sandwich away. His gaze remained on the plate, but Ella doubted he was in intense study of what remained of his food. She was reasonably certain he was lost in thoughts of Cassidy Maxwell.

"I always wondered if you might have had…I don't know, a little crush on her," Ella said, trying to figure out what was going on with Eric and if there was a way around it.

"We grew up together. We were friends. I was five years older than she was—that isn't such a big deal now, but when we were younger it seemed like too much."

"So the two of you never got together romantically?"

"No."

One word, full of sadness, regret…and maybe anger?

"And then you parted ways?" Ella continued to probe, telling herself it was for the greater good.

"You could say that." Eric seemed to be wrestling with himself. But then he continued. "The truth is, Cassidy just disappeared on me. On her own graduation day from Saunders, as a matter of fact. Without a word. A long time passed before I even heard she was in London and by then…" Eric shrugged. "I thought about going after her, seeing if I could find out why she just left like that. But, hey, I figured if she had anything to say to me, she'd have called or written or…something."

"But she didn't."

"Not a word."

Okay, so he wasn't terribly responsive to the course Ella had set them on. But still, with Gilbert Harrison's problems in mind, she persisted.

"Maybe this would give you a reason to finally go after her and find out why she left that way."

Eric shook his head forcefully, laughing a wry, mirthless laugh. "I don't think so."

Ella never gave up without a fight. "You could look Cassidy up," she said with a voice full of intrigue. "Then you could tell her what's going on with Professor Harrison, that he needs her help. It wouldn't be like you were going for any personal reasons. But in the process you might get some questions of your own answered."

"Cassidy and I are history," Eric insisted, not hostilely but as if he knew things she didn't know.

"I didn't say you had to rekindle anything—not even

the friendship, if you don't want to. I'm just saying this could be a way to help Professor Harrison—and solve a few other mysteries."

"He's a good man, Professor Harrison," Eric conceded slowly.

"He really is. And he needs all the help he can get."

Eric glanced away from Ella, out at the other people in the restaurant without focusing on any one of them. But the even deeper crease of his brow let her know he was unwillingly considering her proposal.

Then, just when she was worrying that he was going to refuse her after all, he said, "I *do* have some time off coming. I also have a ton of air miles I should use before I lose them."

A crack in the door…

"And the people working on this for Professor Harrison really want Cassidy Maxwell's help," Ella reiterated so as not to waste what might be an opportunity.

"I don't know," Eric said, clearly wavering again.

This time Ella resisted the urge to say more, not wanting to pressure him unduly. Especially when she had the impression that many things were going through Eric's mind at once. She just kept her fingers crossed that he would make the decision to go to London.

Then, finally, he said, "I suppose I could do it."

Not a lot of enthusiasm, but at that point Ella was willing to take what she could get.

"That would be great. I'm sure it would carry a whole lot more weight for an old friend to go all the way to England to ask for Cassidy's help than for her to just get a phone call or an e-mail from somebody she doesn't even know."

Eric merely nodded, obviously still not thrilled with the whole idea.

But Ella was just happy to have gotten what she needed. What Professor Harrison needed.

"You'll go soon?" she asked.

"As soon as I can make arrangements."

No, he was definitely not doing somersaults of joy at the prospect.

"It really is a big help," Ella assured.

Again he just nodded. Then he raised his wrist to look at his watch and took his napkin from his lap, setting it on the table.

"Stay and finish your lunch, Ella— I'd better get going," he announced.

"I wouldn't want you to be late for your meeting," Ella said even though she was reasonably sure she'd lost him more to the demons she'd resurrected by bringing up Cassidy Maxwell than to work.

Eric stood. "I'll let you know what happens with Cassidy."

"Thanks, I appreciate it. Everyone on Professor Harrison's side will appreciate it."

For the third time Eric only nodded. "It *was* good to see you again, though."

"You, too."

"I'll get this," he said, picking up the check. "It's the least I can do for being bad company."

"You weren't bad company."

"Liar," he accused with a smile, taking the check, anyway.

Ella watched him as he paid their bill near the restaurant's entrance, and as she did she could only hope she hadn't stirred up something she shouldn't have when it came to Eric and Cassidy Maxwell.

But she realized she might have.

Chapter Twelve

"So, Prince Charming, are you ready to take the crown off yet?"

Ella couldn't suppress a smile as she glanced at Jacob, sitting behind the wheel of his Porsche, still wearing the paper crown her niece had insisted he be coronated with and not remove throughout the entire birthday party they'd just left.

"Are you asking me to abdicate my throne?" he inquired with mock solemnity.

Ella laughed. "Far be it from me to make a request like that, no. I was just wondering if you might be tired of the headgear."

The teenagers in the car next to them at a red light did a double take and then burst out laughing. Remaining in character, Jacob gave them an imperial stare and a screwing-in-a-lightbulb wave before the light turned green and he pulled away from the intersection.

Then he breathed a resigned sigh and said, "All right. You may remove my crown."

He leaned to the side enough to accommodate Ella taking it off for him and then straightened again. "But I'll miss it," he lamented.

Another laugh went with a warmth in the vicinity of Ella's heart as it occurred to her that he had taken a giant step tonight. And not only in obviously working to conquer what had seemed to be some initial discomfort at being around so many unfamiliar faces. Jacob had also put effort into winning over her sister, her brother-in-law and her niece by being charming, down-to-earth and by completely indulging Janey, who had fallen in love at first sight with the handsome doctor and—in keeping with the birthday party's princess theme—decreed that he be her prince for the event. Jacob had also taken a giant step with Ella, who was not only grateful for the effort he'd put into the evening but was also impressed, entertained and intrigued even more by the lighter side of the man.

First Champ and now this…

Sitting on one of Janey's miniature chairs at her miniature table—with his knees nearly to his chin—drinking pretend tea. Enduring the three-year-old's nonsensical stories and her endless showing off to him. Feigning interest when Janey displayed and demonstrated for him almost every toy she owned. Letting her hold his hand to drag him away from the adults each time the whim struck for the princess to have the attendance of her prince. Not only catering to her and humoring her, but playing the role to the hilt so that Janey could believe he was as enthralled with her as she had been with him....

"You can be kind of goofy," Ella said, not concealing her amazement at that fact.

He gave her a sideways glance. "Didn't think I had it in me, huh?"

"No, I didn't."

"Surprise!" he said with a secret grin that showed her he was pleased to have shocked her.

"It was nice, though," she told him. "Janey adored you."

"How about Janey's aunt? Does she adore me?"

Ella wasn't sure if he was kidding or not. But luckily the drive from Sara's house to Ella's apartment took only ten minutes and they'd reached it by then.

She used that fact to escape a serious answer to his question and to ease into something else.

"Well, Janey's aunt adores you at least enough to have bought your dog a ball of her own. Except that I forgot to grab it when I saw you drive up tonight and came out to meet you, so it's still upstairs."

Which she honestly hadn't intended to use as a device to get him back to her apartment tonight. At least not consciously.

"You bought Champ a ball?"

"One that's just her size."

"Shall I come up and get it?" he asked as he parked the Porsche in front of her building.

"You can. Or, if you're worried about Champ being

alone more tonight and need to get home, I can bring it to the office when I come on Monday night," Ella pointed out, not wanting it to appear that she'd left the ball upstairs as a lure.

"Monday night?" he repeated as if he hadn't realized that would be the next time they would see each other. "Monday night seems like a long time for Champ to wait for her new toy. And I'm sure she's sound asleep and doesn't even know I've been gone."

"Come up, then," Ella said airily, as if she wasn't pleased in the extreme to know that their time together wouldn't end just yet.

She didn't wait for Jacob to open her door, but instead was out of the car by the time he came around to her side.

"I can also offer *real* tea rather than the phantom kind Janey was serving you tonight. Or coffee," Ella informed him as she led the way up the steps to her place and let them both in.

"To tell you the truth I'd just be happy with a glass of ice water after all the candy Janey fed me."

"Ice water it is," Ella responded with another smile at the memory of her niece plying Jacob with treats and him gamely eating all she forced on him.

"Make yourself at home," Ella advised as she dropped her purse on a table near the door and went into the kitchen for two glasses of ice water.

Jacob was sitting on her sofa when she got to the living room and while she could have chosen the chair nearby for herself, she didn't. She sat on the couch, too, far enough away for decorum's sake but angled to face him.

Despite the fact that she'd rarely had her eyes off him all evening, she still felt as if she hadn't gotten her fill of the sight of him, and there was no harm—or so she told herself—in getting to look at him now.

He was dressed in a pair of casual gray slacks and a yellow-and-white pinstriped sport shirt with the sleeves rolled to his elbows—nothing remarkable but he still managed to be a sight to behold with those broad shoulders filling out that shirt to perfection, and the slacks riding his hips close enough to pull her eyes more than once tonight to his rear end.

"Champ's ball," Ella announced, taking it from the coffee table and handing it to him once she was settled and had put her glass down.

"You're right, this is just her size," Jacob agreed, holding the small, squishy toy in one upraised palm before he closed long, thick fingers around it, squeezing it in a motion that, for no reason Ella could fathom, sent chills up her spine. Chills so sensual she felt her nipples suddenly stand at attention within the cups of the silky camisole she wore beneath her lacy cardigan.

Jacob took another drink of his water and set his own glass on the coffee table with Ella's, repositioning himself so that he was turned toward her, too. "Champ will love it," he said as he put the ball into his pants pocket. "She thanks you."

"She's welcome," Ella responded. Then, with that subject exhausted, she returned to their earlier one. "You really impressed me tonight."

"So you *do* adore your liege," he joked.

"Impressed is not the same as *adore,*" she amended, adding facetiously, "My liege."

That made him incline his head as if the title were his due.

Ella smiled again. "I was impressed by your patience with Janey and how easily you got into baseball talk with Andy and his friends, and how much you remembered about Sara—she was very flattered when you told her you recalled that piece she'd written for the Saunders newspaper."

"Did you expect me to stand in a corner and scowl?"

Actually, she'd wondered if he might. But she didn't say that.

"No, but you weren't shy, either, and that was nice." *Shy* being a tactful way of saying she'd been slightly concerned that he might be standoffish.

But maybe she was venturing into things that might not be easy to talk about tactfully, so she veered out of them. "Anyway, thanks for being so good with Janey."

"I could tell how important she is to you. You're very attached to her, aren't you?"

"I am," Ella admitted.

"Did she inspire your determination to have a baby of your own? Even without a husband in the picture?"

"I wanted a baby of my own long before Janey was born, and having a husband in the picture was my problem in the first place."

That confused him and it showed. "Uh…how was having a husband in the picture a problem?"

"I always wanted kids. Always. I started babysitting at thirteen and went on doing it well after my friends had stopped because I just loved children. I wanted to go to college, to be an attorney and have a career, but equal to all of that, I wanted a family and I wanted it as soon as possible."

"Husband or no husband?"

"No, not then. Then I wanted the whole package—husband and kids."

"So you got married."

"Brandon and I met at a prep course for the bar exam. He'd graduated the year before I had and already failed once. We studied together, got to know each other, liked each other, and after the test, he asked me out."

"A two-lawyer family," Jacob said as if that was auspicious. "How long did you date before you tied the knot?"

"A year. And during that whole time I was very vocal about what my goals were—"

"Marriage and kids."

"Exactly."

"And…Brandon? Was that his name?"

"Brandon, yes," Ella confirmed.

"Was that what he wanted, too?"

"I thought so. But looking back—after it was too late—I realized that he never actually said that. He just didn't say he *didn't* want it, so I guess I took it from there and assumed he did. I assumed that when he proposed and I accepted, it was so we could not only begin our life together but our family, too."

"Seems reasonable if you were aboveboard about your own goals."

"I was more than aboveboard about it, we were together when I found a handmade baby quilt at a craft fair and bought it to start my baby hope chest."

"That does seem pretty clear."

Jacob retrieved his glass from the coffee table and took another drink. When he replaced it and settled back again it almost seemed as if he were closer to her than he'd been before.

Ella made some adjustments of her own—kicking off the sandals she had on with her brown drawstring pants and curling her legs partially underneath her. Which coincidentally brought her a bit nearer to him, too.

"So the two of you got married and you figured it would only be a matter of time before you were using that baby quilt," Jacob said to urge her to continue.

"Exactly. I even suggested on our honeymoon that we stop using birth control."

Jacob's eyebrows arched. "That's soon," he said as if it would be too soon for him, too.

"I know," Ella conceded. "And Brandon balked. He said he didn't want to be *that* tied down right off the bat."

"That tied down?" Jacob repeated. "Were those his words?"

"Verbatim. It kind of shocked me, too. I'd seen our getting married as a positive step, not as being *tied down.* But when I took issue with the semantics, Brandon said I was just splitting hairs, that he hadn't meant anything negative, it was just that we were both only in our midtwenties, we'd just finished a whole lot of school, we needed to get our careers started, and it didn't seem like it was a great idea to have a baby nine months from then. I could see his point, so I kept taking the pill."

"What kind of law did our Brandon practice?" Jacob asked.

"Corporate."

"So he *did* pass the bar the second time?"

"Right."

"Okay, so now you've both passed the bar—him on the second try, you on the first—and you've agreed to pay some dues on the career front before starting a family," Jacob summarized.

"Mmm. *Some* dues. I thought a year or so."

"But our Brandon thought differently?"

"I suggested stopping birth control again on our first anniversary, and again he put me off—our careers still weren't stable, we were living in a small apartment, had almost no money in the bank…he had a laundry list of reasons."

"And once more you agreed?"

"Less willingly. The trouble was, that set the course and he kept it up—every time I so much as approached the subject of a baby, he found excuse after excuse to put me off until more than five years had gone by. I was thirty-one by then, I knew time was against me, and I just plain didn't want to wait any more. So I finally insisted."

"But he still wasn't enthusiastic?" Jacob guessed.

"You could say that," Ella answered, unable to keep an edge of residual anger out of her tone. "He said that whether I was ready or not, he wasn't, and if I was determined to do this, any kids we had would be my responsibility. That I'd better not expect him to change diapers or wipe noses or coach Little League."

Jacob's eyebrows arched a second time. "Nice."

"I know, it seems like a rotten beginning to having a family and it certainly wasn't a fulfillment of my fantasy of the way it would be. But I honestly thought that once we had a baby, Brandon would fall in love with it like any father. And if he never changed a diaper or wiped a nose, that was okay with me. I was just glad that I could finally go off the pill and we could start trying."

"Only you didn't conceive," Jacob said.

"No. I didn't," Ella confirmed, her voice catching slightly.

"Somehow I can't picture good old Brandon eager for the infertility ordeal."

"It was like pulling teeth to get him to do any of the tests or the procedures or any of the different things we were advised to try to improve our chances."

"But he did them?"

"Some of the simpler things. A lot of them he refused to be a part of."

Ella had to blink back the sudden moisture that flooded her eyes as she recalled how difficult it had been to go through what she'd gone through, not only without her husband's support, but having to beg and plead for even minimal cooperation on his part.

Jacob must have seen the tears despite the fact that she didn't let them fall. His tone was conciliatory when he said, "Infertility itself puts a strain on a marriage. Add a reluctant partner to the mix and…"

"To call it a strain on the marriage—and on the relationship—is an understatement," Ella finished for him. "Brandon complained that I was obsessed with baby making, that I wasn't paying enough attention to him. He said I was ruining his life. Taking all the fun out of it—his life *and* making love. That I was neglecting him." Ella's voice caught in her throat and she had to clear it before she could go on. "I didn't think I was neglecting him. I tried really hard not to. But who knows? Maybe I was…."

The doubt Ella still carried with her echoed in her voice, and Jacob must have heard and recognized it. He reached over and took one of her hands into both of his.

The gesture drew her gaze, and the sight of those big, capable hands cupping hers, the warmth, the strength of having them envelop her, helped more than he probably knew. Even as it sent yet another wave of those sensual chills along the surface of her skin.

Then he said, "Not a lot of the husbands of my patients are like this, Ella, but I've run into a few. More than a fair share of them give me the impression that they're immature. Irresponsible. That they don't want to share anything—their wives, their lives, the spotlight. They definitely don't want the work and worry that come with parenting. I usually don't encourage too much in the way of treatment because they're uncooperative and, to tell you the truth, the marriages usually don't survive—they end either before the woman gets pregnant at all or not long after they have a baby."

"Well, mine ended before. Brandon had an affair and announced that he'd found someone who was more interested in him than in kids."

Jacob nodded as if that didn't come as a shock to him, either.

"And there I was, having wasted what were probably my most fertile years," she said with a full measure of her own regrets in her voice. She looked up at Jacob then, finding his expression compassionate and understanding. "But it didn't change how much I wanted a baby, and so I decided not to waste any more time," she concluded quietly.

He gave her a gentle smile. "I know this is no consolation at all, but I see something good coming out of a lot of bad. And I can't hate that this is how things played out."

Ella didn't understand that and her confusion must have been in her expression because he clarified.

"One step in any other direction and I probably would never have met you."

Now she knew what he'd meant, and strangely, there was more consolation in his words than he knew. Enough to lighten the darker emotions this topic brought out in Ella and make her feel a whole lot better.

Especially when his hands tightened around hers and sent more of those chills running through her.

"I *am* a big believer that things work out for the best," she said, looking into those almost-purple eyes that seemed to reach out and touch her as surely as his hands had.

And while talking about her shattered marriage and her problems conceiving were an unlikely segue, it still felt like just the right moment for him to lean forward and kiss her.

Ella allowed her eyes to drift closed and gave in to his kiss. It was astonishing how easy it was to let the moment take her to an entirely different place than she'd been only seconds before. To take her to a place where it just felt good to be with Jacob. Where nothing else seemed to matter.

He released her hand from one of his and brought it to her cheek to tilt her face slightly more toward him as he deepened the kiss, parting his lips and waiting for her to answer by parting hers, too.

He didn't have much of a wait because Ella's lips seemed to part all by themselves, not only in answer but in invitation as well. In fact, it was Ella's tongue that took the next step, teasing him, running the tip faintly along the edge of his teeth.

She felt him smile as his tongue met hers and took command, tip to tip, circling and taunting just before making a full-out onslaught to chase it firmly in her direction.

His other arm went around her, pulling her much, much nearer as they both slipped lower on the sofa until their heads ended up pillowed against the rear cushions. In fact, he pulled her so close that her breasts brushed his chest. And if she'd thought her nipples had hardened before, it was nothing in comparison to the taut crests that nudged at him now.

Mouths were wider—as wide as they could be— and tongues toyed as that kiss became infused with a fervor that raised Ella's hands to Jacob's chest where she drank in the feel of him through her palms and was compelled to seek more.

Big biceps. Broad shoulders. Thick, sharply corded neck. Hard, strong back…

The heat of his body warmed his shirt, warmed her, and made her start to imagine running her hands over his skin alone, without that shirt as a filter.

Retracing her path, she found the buttons that ran down the placket of his sport shirt. Ignoring thoughts of whether or not she should do it, she unfastened the buttons with speed and dipped inside.

Why was it that a man's skin felt different from a woman's? She didn't know the answer but she reveled in the feel of that difference, the firm smoothness that was sleek and sexy without being soft.

But as good as he felt beneath her hands, it still didn't satisfy all that was driving her, all that was driving her body even as his mouth plundered hers and his hands plunged into her hair to brace her head against the on-slaught.

Her own clothes seemed in the way now. Keeping her breasts isolated when they didn't want to be. Bound, when they wanted to be unleashed. Ignored, when they were screaming for attention.

Her hands went up and over his shoulders again, dragging his shirt partially off and bringing her own chest into contact with his, where the tiny knots of her nipples made their presence known.

Jacob must have felt them because a guttural groan rumbled from far in his throat as if he were being tortured, and he drew both of his hands to the sides of her breasts.

But that was as far as he went. Massaging, kneading

those lateral mounds like a sneak preview of things to come, until he'd raised the bar on her desire. Then he shifted just enough to insinuate one of his hands between their bodies, finally taking one breast fully into his grasp, proving the wait had been worth it, as long, thick fingers worked her flesh and made her want even more.

His hand deserted her then, but only for the briefest time so he could slip under her cardigan and camisole at once and find that bare globe that waited within, swollen and almost throbbing with the demand for his touch. His poised, powerful touch...

If her nipple had ever grown as hard as it did right then, Ella hadn't been aware of it. It was like a diamond in his palm and he knew just how to handle it. Tugging and teasing in turns. Softly stroking with only his fingertips, then rolling it just so, until a moan escaped Ella's throat and her spine arched and tightened some kind of connection between her breasts and much lower regions of her body.

And it surprised her. Shocked her enough to make her take stock of what she was doing. Of whether or not she *should* be doing it.

And once that stock had been taken, she wasn't so sure.

This wasn't what she was supposed to be doing; she knew that. It wasn't what she was supposed to be focusing on. And losing her focus was something she swore she'd never let happen again. Not when, once before, she'd let her feelings for a man get between herself and her goals, and it had damaged her chances of ever reaching that goal.

And while nothing but being there with Jacob, having him touch her, kiss her, had seemed to matter before, she suddenly remembered that there *was* something else that mattered to her. Something that couldn't be put off. Not for another man. Not even for the want of another man. Especially a man she wasn't altogether sure of because he was so difficult to get a handle on....

"No, wait..." she said, breaking away from that kiss, leaning back from that hand she craved to feel everywhere on her body. "Maybe we're kind of jumping the gun."

Out from under her camisole came his hand and Ella thought that if her breast had had a voice it would have cried out in complaint. But she ignored those physical demands and reminded herself that a cooler head had to prevail. Or at least as cool as her head could be at that moment. Which was not altogether cool at all....

Jacob smiled at her, looking slightly sheepish but hardly shamefaced. "Well, you *did* buy my dog a present. No good deed can go unpunished," he joked as an excuse.

"Guess that'll teach me," she countered the same way, going with the theme because it was easier than trying to make clear to him why she'd let this go so far and then abruptly stopped it when none of it was altogether clear to her.

He kissed her again, maybe to let her know there were no hard feelings for putting an end to what had been happening between them, and then sat up straighter himself, putting more distance between them as he righted his shirt and rebuttoned it.

But after a few minutes of concentrating on that he looked at her again, leveling those amazing blue eyes on her with an expression on his staggeringly attractive face that made her think something had just occurred to him. "Monday night?" he said.

Ella knew he was referring to her earlier mention that that was the next time she'd see him.

"For acupuncture," she elaborated.

"Why does that seem like decades away?"

It did to her, too, but before she could find a way to say it, he said, "I still own the old family home—it's also not far from Saunders's campus. I like to get away there on the weekend—if I don't, I usually end up going into the office to do paperwork. I'm having the place remodeled and I'm headed there tomorrow to check on the progress, spend the night. There are at least two bedrooms with their own baths that are finished and usable..." He paused as if to let all of that information sink in, then he added, "If you don't have plans for the next two days, maybe you'd come with me?"

Ella's mind—and body—were still reeling from what they'd just done, from the unsatisfied desires running like crazed gremlins through her, and the invitation took her aback slightly.

He was asking her to go away with him for the weekend....

There was no doubt that she shouldn't.

So why did she hear herself say, "Separate rooms?" as if she were considering it?

"With locks on the doors, and you can jam a chair under the handle if you don't think you can trust me."

It was herself she was afraid she couldn't trust.

And yet she said, "It would be nice to get even to the edge of the city for a couple of days. See the campus again. It's been a long time since I've been back."

"A little rest and relaxation. Some good food. Just taking it easy for two days..." he said enticingly. Then he held his hands up, palms outward, and added, "We can even have a three-feet-apart-at-all-times clause, if that would make you feel better. I just want your company."

She shouldn't. She shouldn't. She shouldn't....

"Okay," she heard herself say, anyway. "If you promise we'll be in separate rooms."

"Cross my heart," he swore, using one long index finger to do just that.

He stood then and so did Ella, following him to her door. But once he'd opened it he didn't step outside, he turned back to her with Champ's ball in his hand again—apparently having taken it out of his pocket along the way.

"Want to keep this and give it to Champ yourself?" he asked.

"Sure," she said, taking the small ball back.

The scant brushing of their hands was enough to set everything off in Ella all over again and make her wonder about her decision to go away with him. But it was too late now.

Or so she told herself.

"I'll pick you up about noon. We can have lunch and then make the drive," he said.

"I'll be ready."

He leaned over and kissed her once more, a kiss that still contained a heaping helping of all that had been roused between them so shortly before but that held it in check.

Then he straightened again and said, "Three feet away at all times—beginning tomorrow."

Ella had to smile at the pure mischief in his expression. "Three feet away at all times," she repeated more firmly.

"And separate rooms."

"Absolutely separate," she insisted.

"Absolutely," he agreed with a glint in his eyes.

But then he left, and she closed the door and dropped her forehead to it.

Wondering as she did if she'd completely lost her mind.

What other explanation could there be for agreeing to go away for the weekend with someone she'd just come so close to crossing the line for?

Someone who, try as she might, she had so little resistance to.

Chapter Thirteen

"I know what you're thinking and you're wrong," Jacob said to Champ the next morning.

Jacob was packing the duffel bag he used for weekend trips to his old family home. The bag was on his bed and so was the tiny schnauzer, perched atop his pillow, staring at him—head cocked to one side, one ear raised in the air.

"You're thinking that I'm letting down my guard with this woman. That I've never taken anyone else to the house. That this whole thing about feeling inclined to invite Ella because not seeing her for two days seemed like too much time away from her is odd. And an indication that I'm getting in over my head. But you're wrong," he repeated as he paid more attention than usual to what clothes he was bringing with him.

Champ barked one bark as if she knew he was talking to her, she understood what he was telling her and was maintaining her opinion no matter what he said.

"I'm not letting down my guard or getting in over my head," Jacob argued. "So what if I have a good time with Ella? I'm entitled. That doesn't mean anything but that I have a good time with her. Which is why I asked her to the house. It doesn't mean I expect anything from her or that I'm depending on her—not even for my entertainment, because if she'd said no to this weekend I would still have gone to the house, exactly as I'd planned."

Although, he knew it wouldn't have been the same. That he wouldn't have been looking forward to it the way he was.

And he also knew—despite the fact that he didn't want to confess it to Champ—that if Ella *had* turned him down for the weekend but still been available to see him *in* town, he might have changed his plans....

"Bad sign," he muttered.

Apparently his tone was ominous enough to make Champ think she'd done something wrong, because her raised ear folded over and she gave a pouty, defensive sort of bark.

"No, you're a good girl," Jacob was quick to console the puppy, reaching over to scratch the side of her neck with one index finger the way she liked.

But just *how* bad a sign was it that he could well have been tempted to alter his plans for a woman? he asked himself.

It wasn't *too* bad, he decided after a moment of contemplation and more Champ scratching. Because even if that's what had happened, even if once it had happened Ella had backed out and left him hanging, he would still have had work he could have done. He wouldn't have been left alone, with time on his hands and nothing to do. He'd have adjusted. Adapted.

And he'd have known never to change his plans for her again.

That rationale made him feel better, and he stopped petting Champ to return to his packing. And to talking to his puppy.

"You and I would have done just fine," he said as if the dog had been privy to his train of thought. "There've been other women, you know? Not lately, since you've been around, but here and there. And believe me, I know where to draw the line with them. I know how far to let things go before I cool it. So I'll know with this one, too. It doesn't matter that I'm taking her to the house."

So why did it seem to matter?

Maybe just because he'd never done it before.

Or maybe because things with Ella—what he was feeling in regards to Ella—were different…

"Okay, so maybe there's no maybe about it," he said to himself rather than to Champ, admitting it reluctantly, carefully, and not at all happily that things with Ella *were* different.

Admitting it without any kind of understanding of how it could be true. Of how he could have let it happen. Already.

Yes, she was beautiful and bright and witty and she never let him put anything past her. Yes, she was a challenge. She was funny. She was clever. She was stimulating. And sexier than hell. But still, *feelings?* Did he actually have *feelings* for her?

That possibility hit him so hard he stopped packing, picked up Champ as if she were a security blanket he needed to hold close to him and sat on the bed.

Feelings…

For Ella…

"Let's think about this," he said as if he were enlisting Champ in a problem-solving process.

Exactly what *feelings* did he have for Ella?

He liked her—that was a feeling. He enjoyed her company—that was another feeling. He was attracted to her—three for three. He was drawn to her, to spending time with her, and he missed her when he wasn't with her or even when he knew he wouldn't be with her. Feelings. All feelings.

But not feelings that couldn't be controlled and, more important, not feelings that controlled him.

And that was the key, he told himself. That none of the feelings that Ella inspired controlled him. And that now that he recognized that he *had* feelings for her, he *could* control them.

"Recognizing the problem," he informed Champ. "The first step in a solution."

And what was the solution?

The most obvious, of course, would be to end things with Ella now. To nip their relationship in the bud. No Ella, no feelings, no risk, no problem.

"I could pick up the phone right now, call her, tell her I've had an emergency and can't go to the house after all, then go without her. She'd never know the difference, and when she comes into the office Monday night, I could make sure I don't even see her. By the time she's ready for my medical treatment, she'll just be another patient."

Champ had begun fighting with a button on his shirt and ignored that suggestion.

It didn't take Jacob long to ignore it, too. Or at least to discount it.

He didn't want to call off this weekend. To go alone to the house. To steer clear of Ella until she became just another patient.

And he didn't think that was what he had to do.

He'd always been able to keep his feelings and the situations with other women under control, and he just needed to do that same thing with Ella, he assured himself. As long as he did that, he could still enjoy her company. Get to know her a little more. Spend time with her. Now that he knew there was the potential for a problem—

"Because really, isn't that all this is? The *potential* for a problem, not really a problem yet?"

And now that he knew there was the potential for a problem, he could make sure the problem never occurred.

"Forewarned is forearmed."

He just wouldn't let his *feelings* go any further.

He could enjoy Ella's company. He could enjoy Ella. Knowing full well that this, like his relationships with other women, was a temporary situation. A situation that would end before long and provide a little distraction, a little entertainment, a little pleasure, in the meantime.

"And that's all there is to it."

Even if he was taking her to his family home for the weekend.

"So I'm varying from the beaten path this time. It's only slightly. And it means nothing," he assured Champ, lifting her up to look into her eyes. "It doesn't mean a thing. You really were wrong."

Champ licked his nose, and Jacob took that as the seal of approval for the conclusion he'd reached.

"Now let's get this packing finished so we can pick up Ella and put this show on the road," he said, setting the schnauzer back on the mattress and going on about his business.

All the while pretending not to notice how eager he was to have Ella beside him in the Porsche on their way to two days alone together.

And pretending as well not to notice just how difficult it was for him to keep his eagerness contained in any way.

"The food's not only good, but they also have patio dining so we can bring Champ. If I leave her in the car while we eat we might find holes chewed in my seats."

Jacob was outlining his suggestion for lunch at a bistro.

"Besides," Ella added, "it would be a shame to waste a day like today eating inside."

As he'd promised, Jacob had picked her up at noon on Saturday, and the early September weather couldn't have been better. Eighty degrees. No wind. Not a cloud in a sky so blue it looked as if it had come straight from an artist's palette.

If Ella were more superstitious she might have believed her weekend away with Jacob was being blessed. As it was she just hoped she wasn't making a mistake to be doing this.

But not even an almost-sleepless night of fretting over the wisdom—or lack of it—in going with him to his house near Saunders had been enough to make her get up this morning and beg off.

Because, wise or unwise, she still wanted to be with him to such a degree that she hadn't been able to force herself to cancel. Instead she'd reminded herself that he'd guaranteed her a separate bedroom. She'd told herself that if he'd been simply a male friend, she wouldn't have hesitated to accept an invitation to go away for a relaxing weekend. And she'd sworn that she wouldn't do anything stupid. She wouldn't do anything but enjoy seeing the campus again, enjoy Jacob's house, enjoy his company—platonically, purely platonically—all the while keeping in mind that she was doing nothing more than biding her time until she could get pregnant, have her baby and begin her real life.

"Sandra and David Westport are here," Jacob said, interrupting her thoughts as he parked the Porsche near the restaurant.

Ella glanced in the direction of the tables behind a wrought-iron railing where many people occupied café chairs around small round tables that made the whole scene look like something from a Paris street.

"You said this place was near their store," Ella reminded. "They must have come for their lunch break."

"And to see Rachel James. That's her with them. She's been working with us on Gilbert's behalf but she wasn't at the meeting the other night."

"She's the one everyone is worried about," Ella supplied to let him know she'd been paying attention.

"Right."

"She doesn't look any too happy," Ella observed of the pretty woman, with curly black hair who was with the Westports.

"She doesn't, does she?" Jacob agreed

Champ was riding in Ella's lap, so it required some maneuvering to gather her purse from the floorboard and pick up the puppy to get out of the car. It allowed Jacob time to come around and open her door for her.

He was dressed in a black mock-turtleneck T-shirt and a pair of jeans. It was the first time she'd seen him in such casual clothes, and he was definitely a sight to behold. The T-shirt revealed his expansive shoulders, chest, back, and bulging biceps, leaving no doubt how impressive they were, and the jeans were nothing less than a masterpiece hugging narrow hips, thick thighs and a butt good enough to stop traffic.

"Here, let me take the beast," he said, once Ella was on the sidewalk with him, reaching a big hand to cup Champ's belly and lift her to carry against his flat middle.

The Westports spotted them coming and called to

them, but Ella noticed that the woman with them never cracked a smile. In fact, her eyes scanned the area as if she were searching for an escape route.

There was a gate in the wrought-iron railing, and Ella, Jacob and Champ went in through it rather than using the front door of the bistro.

"Join us," Sandra invited after they'd all greeted each other and introduced Rachel James to Ella.

"It looks like you're about finished," Jacob observed of their mostly eaten meals.

"We still have a little left to polish off. We'll get our waiter over to take your orders. Otherwise you'll have to put your name on the list and stand around for half an hour," David said, nodding in reference to the people forced to clog the entrance until tables were free.

"One of you can have my chair," Rachel James offered, standing as if she had discovered the escape Ella had thought she'd been looking for. "I *am* finished and I have somewhere I should get to."

She took money from her purse, but David Westport waved away the notion of her paying for her lunch. "We insisted on this today. It's our treat."

"Thanks," Rachel James said, still seeming very intense to Ella as she told her she was happy to have met her.

"Don't forget," Sandra said to the woman, "Gilbert isn't the only person we'd pitch in to help. If you need something…anything—"

"I really am fine," Rachel said, sounding not fine at all.

"We'll let you know when we're going to meet again," David contributed.

"It seems like everything is under control. You don't really need me. But I'm sure I'll talk to you soon," she said as if she didn't have any intention of talking to anyone but needed an exit line. And having given it, she did just that—she made haste toward the same gate Ella and Jacob had used to enter the patio dining area and left.

"That doesn't sound like it went well," Jacob said.

"It didn't," Sandra Westport confirmed.

"Sandra had trouble just getting Rachel to agree to see us today," David contributed. "And when we told her we could tell that something was bothering her, she denied it. She wouldn't tell us what was wrong, or what was going on with her, or anything."

"She said she's just busy," Sandra supplied. "But you saw her, Jacob, she doesn't even look like herself."

"She seemed a little frazzled," Jacob said. "And now she doesn't want to work on helping Gilbert?"

"I guess not," David answered.

"We can do it without her—especially if Ella's friend gets Cassidy Maxwell to pitch in—but I'm still worried that something is wrong with Rachel," Sandra said, sounding very motherly.

"It's tough to say what's going on behind the scenes with anyone. Particularly if they don't want you to know," Jacob pointed out, making Ella think of the youthful secrets he'd worked so hard to keep himself.

But with the subject of Rachel unable to be explored further, Sandra and David turned their attention to Champ.

Champ, who was sitting perched on Jacob's lap, taking in all the sights and scents around her as if she had every right to be at a dining table, was oblivious to the travails of the humans. Or to those of the woman who had just so hastily left them all behind.

Chapter Fourteen

During her days at Saunders, Ella had noticed the three-story stone-castlelike house on her daily drive to the campus because it was imposing and impossible not to see standing tall and proud behind the huge poplar trees that lined its circular drive. But she'd never known who it belonged to.

"*This* is your house?" she marveled as Jacob drove up the brick-paved lane that he'd turned onto from the main street. "Were there English lords in your background?"

Jacob laughed. "Anglophiles, maybe, but no lords."

"It even has a turret."

"And an elevator that hasn't worked in years. The whole third floor is closed off for the time being while I renovate the living areas on the first floor and the bedrooms and baths on the second. The turret is more decorative than anything. From the inside it just gives alcoves to the rooms in that section of the house but small, curved alcoves are mostly useless."

The grounds needed work, too, but Ella didn't mention it as they got out of the car.

"You can set Champ down. She'll just make a pit stop and go up to the house, she knows the routine," Jacob informed Ella.

She did as she was told, watching as the tiny black schnauzer did just as her owner had said she would.

Jacob wouldn't let Ella carry her own overnight bag and brought both it and his duffel to the oversize front door that was arched at the top as if it actually was the entry to a castle.

"What do you say I give you the nickel tour, we leave our things packed and take Champ for a walk on campus? We can poke our heads into Gilbert's office, see if he's around, just to say hello?" Jacob said as he unlocked the door.

Ella felt her stomach clench at the thought of seeing the man who had rescued her again. The man whose secret she'd now revealed. "Do you think Professor Harrison will be working this late on a Saturday afternoon?"

"I think work is about all he does anymore," Jacob said, pushing the door open and waiting for Ella to go in ahead of him—following Champ who waited for no one before hopping across the threshold as if she, rather than Jacob, owned the place.

The smell of fresh paint greeted them when they

stepped into the sprawling entry, facing a huge staircase that curved in a semicircle to the second floor. To the right was a formal living room two times larger than Ella's entire apartment, adorned with sawhorses, tools, buckets and debris. And to the left was an ornately carved, closed double door.

"That's the den," Jacob said as if he knew she was wondering. "It's finished, so I shut the doors to keep the construction dust out of it. It's nice, though. There's a fireplace and a full entertainment center if we want to rent a movie or listen to music or whatever tonight."

He'd set their luggage on the floor and opened the doors as he talked. Even though Ella didn't go into the den she could see a big-screen TV, a large, dark brown, comfortable-looking sofa and two matching chairs, along with rich paneled walls and floor-to-ceiling bookshelves.

"Come on, we'll make the loop down here and then go upstairs. The kitchen is in back," Jacob announced, leading her down the corridor beside the staircase and pointing out the ongoing repairs taking place in the formal dining room that occupied the space between the living room and the kitchen.

The kitchen had obviously already been remodeled. It was opulent with a rustic red ceramic tile floor, black granite countertops over dark oak cupboards, and a wealth of the most modern appliances to be had—including an enormous stainless steel refrigerator.

"We should be well stocked with food and drink. I have a service that preps the place for me before my weekends and cleans up after them."

"Great," Ella muttered, taking in the elegant beauty

of the kitchen while noting that it definitely didn't have any lived-in touches to make it homey.

From there he showed her the games room, the screening room, the maid's quarters—all of them in different stages of construction disarray—before they returned to the entry.

"You'll have to give Champ a lift up the steps, she's too small to manage them on her own," Jacob said as he retrieved the luggage and headed for the staircase.

Ella obliged the small dog who had been following them as if she were part of the tour group, carrying her as she and Jacob climbed the steps side by side.

At the first landing they entered a circular common space from which six doors opened.

"These are the bedrooms, each with a bath of its own," he explained. Then, with a nod in the direction of the nearest door to his right and a second nod to the nearest door to his left, he said, "That room is mine and you can take the other one. See? Even more than three feet apart. At all times."

Ella smiled at his referral to the promise he'd made to get her to agree to this weekend, and turned to the door on the left, opening it and going in as he followed with her bag.

As with the other rooms that were complete, the bedroom was spacious and well appointed with a queen-size bed backed by an ornate Victorian headboard. There was also a matching bureau, vanity and dresser, along with a cheval mirror in the far corner.

"The bathroom is through there," Jacob said, nodding this time toward the door beside the tallboy bureau.

Then he set her overnight case on the bench at the foot of the bed. "I'll drop my stuff in the other room, grab Champ's leash, and we can meet downstairs in a few minutes?"

"Sounds good," Ella answered. She handed Champ to him when he held out a hand for the pup and then he left, closing the door behind him as if to prove she had all the privacy she wanted.

She *did* want privacy, she thought as she reminded herself of her vow to keep this weekend platonic.

And the fact that she couldn't keep her eyes off Jacob's rear end in those jeans as he walked out of the room was the reason she *needed* that reminder.

Fall semester had only begun the past week at Saunders, so the campus was alive with students when Ella, Jacob and Champ walked from Jacob's family home to the still-summer-lush green lawns that surrounded the university.

Groups sat at the foot of tall trees chatting and enjoying the warm weather and the camaraderie, and the whole scene brought fond memories back to Ella.

"Gilbert's office is still in the same place," Jacob informed her as they crossed to the building that had always housed it, drawing several looks and laughs at the tiny schnauzer who pranced proudly on a leash that only accentuated just how small she was.

When they reached the building, Jacob picked up Champ to take her inside with them.

Ella couldn't help laughing at the spectacle of the big man holding the tiny dog close to his face and whispering to her to be quiet or she would get them kicked out because only dogs aiding the handicapped were allowed.

Champ responded with one muffled yip as if to challenge his authority but then merely went along for the ride.

Jacob and Ella were two doors down from Gilbert Harrison's office when the older man himself stepped out into the corridor, closing and locking the door before Jacob said, "Gilbert!" to alert him to their presence.

Ella was surprised to see her old teacher and advisor looking as haggard as he did when he raised his gaze to them.

"Jacob," he said in acknowledgment.

"And Ella Gardner, remember her?" Jacob said as they joined the professor at his door.

Gilbert Harrison's eyes moved to Ella for the first time, and recognition dawned. "Of course I remember Ella," he said. But he didn't sound—or look—too happy to realize that's who she was. In fact, he seemed wary of her.

"It's been a long time, Professor Harrison," she said with some reserve of her own, feeling awkward. And guilty.

"Gilbert, please," the older man requested. "Times have changed."

And so had he, apparently. Ella could see for herself what Jacob had referred to as Gilbert Harrison not being the man he used to be. The spark the professor had always had that had made him someone students wanted to be around seemed to have been extinguished. If that was a result of what the administration was doing to him, it made Ella all the more outraged.

"I brought Ella to the house this weekend and we just wanted to stop in and say hello," Jacob explained then.

Gilbert Harrison nodded but still didn't appear too enthusiastic.

"I've told her what's going on here, between you and the school bigwigs," Jacob told him. "I thought you might want to know that Ella is in contact with someone who may be able to reach Cassidy Maxwell so we can enlist her to the cause, too."

Ella thought that her former professor's expression tensed even more at that news.

"Cassidy Maxwell? Ahh... Well, I don't know about that. I hate to have her dragged into this business—"

"I'm sure that isn't how she'll look at it," Ella said.

"No? Well...yes, I guess," the older man stammered as if he just didn't know what to say. Then he looked at his wristwatch and cut things short. "I'm sorry I can't stay and talk. I have an appointment I have to get to. Will you excuse me?"

"Of course," Jacob said.

"Good to see you both," Gilbert called in parting as he hurried to leave them behind in much the way Rachel James had scurried from the restaurant table earlier in the day, disappearing as fast as he could around a corner and down the stairs.

"I don't think it *was* good to see us," Ella observed quietly. "At least, I don't think it was good to see me."

"Gilbert is under a lot of stress right now."

"He remembered, though," Ella insisted. "He remembered me and I'm sure he remembered that I know that he's secretly the benefactor. And when you all confront him with it, he's going to know that I'm the one who told you. Who didn't keep my word to him."

"It's okay," Jacob said comfortingly. "He'd have to know you only broke your promise to help him."

"I don't know what I expected when you said you wanted us to look him up today. I guess maybe I thought I could somehow convey something to him that would let him know—when he found out I blabbed—that I only did it with his best interests in mind. But I certainly didn't pull that off, did I?"

"He didn't give you the chance to pull *anything* off. He was in a hurry."

"To get away from me."

"Or to get to an appointment, the way he said."

Ella didn't actually believe that, but she nodded, realizing that her guilt was her own to bear.

Jacob must have seen through it, though, because he put an arm around her shoulders and pulled her close to his side in a consoling hug.

"It's okay. You did the right thing in telling us. I promise that when we let him know that you did, I'll also let him know that you didn't just *blab* it. That you told us he was the benefactor only reluctantly and for no reason other than to help him."

"Thanks," Ella muttered, meaning it and appreciating Jacob's compassion.

And trying to ignore how nice it was to have his arm around her....

Chapter Fifteen

There was an open-air concert that evening on the Saunders campus. Before it was slated to start, Jacob took Ella—and Champ—to a French restaurant that Ella had only heard about during her days at the university. While the dress code was relaxed enough for them to remain dressed in their casual clothes, it was still a place too expensive for her to have been able to afford on her college budget.

Jacob's healthy tip to the maître d' garnered them a table on the outdoor patio that was far-and-away more elegant than that of the afternoon's bistro. The tip had also provided a discreet turn of the head so Jacob could sneak Champ in with them.

The other diners didn't seem to mind. As Jacob sliced into a rare steak and Ella enjoyed slices of pork tenderloin smothered in an orange-Madeira sauce, several people stopped to admire the adorable puppy.

After dinner they returned to the house for a blanket and Champ's leash and then walked across to the campus again where they spent the rest of the evening sitting on the blanket on the ground, listening to folk and country music provided by talented students.

It was nearly midnight by the time the concert ended and they retraced their steps to the house. Despite the fact that they'd been together since early in the day, Ella found herself loath to say good-night and go off to her room. So when Jacob suggested they finish the bottle of wine they'd taken with them to drink while they listened to the music, she didn't hesitate to agree.

They ended up in the den, sitting on the overly large sofa that was every bit as comfortable as it looked, wineglasses in-hand, while Champ slept like a tired baby on a throw pillow Jacob had set on the floor for her.

"With the exception of feeling bad when we were with Professor Harrison," Ella said, "this has been a great day. Thank you."

"It's good to get away—even if we are only on the far west side of the city," Jacob agreed. "Somehow it still feels like I've left town every time I come here."

Although neither of them had changed clothes for their evening activities, Ella had let her hair down. She'd taken it out of the scrunchee that had contained it all day and allowed it to fall curly and free around her face. And the clean scent of Jacob's cologne wafted around her, intoxicating her more than the wine.

"Is that why you keep this house? Because coming

here gives you a quick getaway?" she asked, trying to drag her mind off his appeal. And her own ever-increasing attraction to him.

"Sometimes I'm not sure *why* I keep it," he seemed to confess. "I considered selling it when my mother died and I inherited it, but...I don't know. I just couldn't do it. Maybe it's some kind of throwback to childhood fantasies about making it a happy family home."

That surprised her. "Really? You have fantasies of a family of your own?"

He smiled a bit wryly. "I used to. That shocks you?"

"I just...I guess I just didn't picture you having fantasies of a wife and kids."

Certainly it seemed as if anyone as accomplished, successful and to-die-for good-looking as he was could have fulfilled that fantasy by now if he harbored it. But then, for all she knew, he might be juggling an entire entourage of women or have been married two or three times.

"Have you ever been married?" she asked then, wanting to know more about the real Jacob.

He smiled a second wry smile. "You have to stop sounding like you can't believe it of me. I could get insulted."

"It isn't that," she assured. "It just struck me that I've thought of you as some kind of crazed workaholic—"

"Crazed workaholic? Like a mad scientist?"

"Sort of. But, hey, maybe you have a wife and kids hidden up on the third floor here, and that's why you have it closed off."

He chuckled. "You've found me out. I keep them sedated when I bring home a date so they don't make any noise."

"Maybe I should go up there and see for myself," Ella threatened in jest.

"But then I'd have to sedate you, too, and what fun would that be?"

"So what *is* the story of your personal life—now and in the past?" she persisted.

"I don't think I care for the crazed part, but workaholic qualifies," he admitted. "That doesn't leave much time for a personal life—past or present, with the exception of the time you and I have spent together lately."

"So you *haven't* ever been married?"

"Never."

"Ever been tempted?"

"Never," he repeated.

"You've never even thought about it?" she asked because he sounded so definitive.

"Never," he said once again.

"Really?"

"Why would I lie?"

"You're over thirty, well established in your career and your community, not *too* hard to look at," she added with a wry smile of her own. "And you've never been so involved with any woman that you've even considered marriage?"

He set his wineglass on the table nearest his end of the couch, and when he turned back toward Ella he was angled in her direction more than he'd been before.

"What part of this aren't you getting?" he asked with

another chuckle. "No, I've never been so involved with any woman that I've considered marriage."

"Have you *had* relationships with women?"

This time he laughed out loud—a rich sound that seemed to bounce off the paneled walls. "If you're wondering if I'm either a virgin or gay, the answer to both is no. Which I would think you had gathered along the way," he added with an expression of pure deviltry.

But Ella wasn't going to be derailed by his charm when she was intent on delving into this portion of him and his life.

"So you have had relationships with women," she said.

"Of course. As a matter of fact, unless I'm mistaken, you're a woman and I'm having a relationship with you."

And he was clearly enjoying his game of cat and mouse. Still, Ella was tenacious. "But nothing has ever come of any of those…other…relationships?"

"Nothing as serious as considering marriage."

"Have you had *long-term* relationships?"

"Nothing that's lasted years and years. But I've seen a few women for several months. A hair shy of a year once."

"Why not longer?" Ella inquired, knowing she was being nosy but not caring.

Jacob shrugged his mile-wide shoulders, and she could see the muscles bunch beneath the black knit of his shirt. But she tried to focus on what he was saying rather than on how good—and sexy—even such an inconsequential movement could be.

"I don't know why I haven't been with anyone for

any long stretch of time," he said. "It just hasn't happened."

"Because the women break up with you or because you break up with them?" That really was nosy and it made her wonder if it was time to curb the wine consumption that might be contributing to her loose lips. So she followed his lead and deposited her glass on the matching table at her end of the sofa. Also readjusting her position afterward to face him more than she was before.

"There haven't been a whole lot of big breakups," he said after a moment's consideration. "Things have rarely gone to the point where that's necessary. I've only been through a single ugly breakup scene."

"With?"

"A woman named Janine. She was a pediatrician I worked with on some high-risk deliveries. She took care of the babies as soon as they were born, so she was in the delivery room with me. We got to know each other some. We had a lot in common. Dating came from that."

"How long did you see each other?"

"That was the relationship that lasted almost a year. In fact, it was the approach of the anniversary of our first date that caused the ending rift."

"How?"

"She wanted to have The Talk—that was what she called it. I didn't know what she meant."

Ella couldn't help smiling at his cluelessness. "What *did* she mean?"

"The Talk was about where the relationship was going. How I felt about her. If we had a future together."

That had been Ella's first guess. "Uh-huh. And?"

"And nothing. I liked Janine well enough. We had some fun. But that was as far as I was willing for it to go. She wanted commitment, marriage, kids. She wanted it all."

"And you didn't have fantasies of that anymore?" Ella asked, referring to the comment that had gotten them into this subject in the first place.

"That's what childhood fantasies are—things you only have in childhood. Things you outgrow. But Janine and I were just seeing each other when we had a little time off. It wasn't anything serious," he said, sounding slightly defensive now rather than playful. "It never crossed my mind that there was any more to it than that."

"But Janine didn't see your relationship as nothing more than a time filler."

"What she said she *saw* was that I kept everyone—including her—outside of some kind of imaginary circle I've erected around myself like a force field."

"Was she right?" Ella asked quietly, thinking that while he had definitely been distant at first, it had seemed as if that distance had lessened during the time they'd shared. Or was that only in her own imagination?

"I suppose there was some merit to Janine's point of view," he conceded. "I don't let a lot of people in. But I'm busy, and work has always come first. Plus I'm self-sufficient and very adept at being alone—maybe from early training."

"Or maybe what your early training taught you is to keep up that force field to protect yourself," Ella suggested. "That if you don't let anyone get past it, you don't risk them disappointing you or leaving you, the way your parents did. You don't risk being hurt."

He gave her a half grin. "I thought you were a lawyer, not a shrink."

And she thought she'd hit on the biggest secret Jacob Weber carried: that his arrogance and prickly disposition hadn't only kept the world from knowing he was alone when he was a teenager or that there was a softer, more vulnerable side to him now; they made sure that history couldn't repeat itself and cause him the same kind of pain his parents' neglect and abandonment had caused him.

Ella's heart went out to this big, tough, gorgeous man who had been so deeply hurt by his own family. This man who had led such a solitary life. A life so unlike what anyone believed he led, cutting himself off from so much.

"I don't think it takes a shrink to see that you don't let anyone get too close," Ella said after a moment of her own ruminations.

Jacob raised an arm to the top of the sofa back and ran his index finger along her hairline, smiling at her in a whole new way, a way that was mischievous and ornery. A smile that had returned to playfulness but with a sexy bent to it now.

"Seems like I've let you get pretty close," he said in a much quieter voice, his tone intimate and very sincere.

So maybe she hadn't been imagining that the distance his surliness put between them had decreased.

"Are you just trying to seduce me?" she felt inclined to ask.

"I promised I wouldn't, remember?"

But oh, how seductive that deep, raspy voice sounded.

"You also promised to stay at least three feet away at all times, and no one could get a yardstick between us right now."

"Shall I move?"

He was rubbing her cheek with the back of his fingers. Barely. His touch a mere whisper against her skin. And yet the thought of making him remove it was not a welcome one.

Ella took a deep breath and sighed. "No," she said almost inaudibly.

"Shall we go up to our separate rooms and lock ourselves in?"

Another unwelcome thought.

"No."

"Because it was you who didn't want us too close last night, if I recall," he reminded her. "And if that's still how you feel, that *is* what I agreed to and I'll stick to it."

But when she considered whether or not that *was* how she still felt, she discovered that it wasn't. Actually, if she were to be honest with herself, she hadn't really wanted them to be at any kind of distance the previous evening, either. She'd just thought that he could be a distraction from her goal.

Only, tonight they were on sort of a minivacation. A time when other things were put on hold. When things like goals weren't forgotten, just temporarily, briefly, set aside.

"It wasn't that I didn't want us to be too close last night," she corrected him.

"What was it, then?"

"I just thought a cool head should prevail."

"And tonight?"

Tonight her head wasn't any cooler than the rest of her. Not when all it was taking to raise her temperature, to make her want him, was to have him nearby, caressing her face the way he was.

"Tonight…" she said, repeating the word but not knowing what else to say.

"Do you want *me* to try to have the cooler head tonight?" he offered.

She knew without a doubt that if she told him she *did* want him to have the cooler head he would take his hand away from her cheek. He wouldn't come so much as an inch nearer. He wouldn't kiss her. He wouldn't do a single thing. A single thing she wanted him to do.

And no amount of telling herself she *should* tell him to have the cooler head, to save her from herself, could force her to say it.

Instead she suddenly gave in to what she'd been fighting since the night before. She gave in to what she wanted.…

She looked up into those eyes that were almost purple, into that face that was so handsome she could hardly believe it, and she reached a hand to the side of his head, to the short bristles of his chestnut hair. "Maybe not *too* cool," she whispered.

His smile this time was small and pleased and overflowing with an appeal that—all by itself—awakened things inside her that had obviously not been sleeping too soundly.

He laid his palm to her cheek then, leaned forward and kissed her. Primly. Properly. In no hurry. Yet with a simmering sensuality that couldn't be mistaken. That had to be surrendered to.

And this time Ella was willing to surrender to it.

She kissed him back, closing her eyes and allowing herself to be set adrift on the meeting of seeking mouths.

When his lips parted so did hers. When his tongue came to reacquaint itself with hers she greeted him in kind. And that was all it took to put aside thoughts of the past and the future, thoughts of force fields and protective dispositions and eventual goals. Thoughts of everything but the fact that she was there with this man who ignited things inside her that she hadn't even been aware she was capable of before meeting him. This man she simply felt like giving herself over to to-night.

So that was what she decided to do.

The hand she'd run through his hair moments before dropped down to stroke his neck, and she didn't resist when he wrapped his arm around her and pulled her nearer. She let her other arm go around him, too, molding her hand to the solid wall of his back as mouths opened even wider and tongues became playful and bold.

Bold enough to lend some courage to Ella, who was in the throes of a sudden urge to rid Jacob of the T-shirt that had only whetted her appetite with what was hidden beneath it.

She grasped it where it was tucked into his jeans and tugged until it was free, then she pulled it upward, waiting to see if he would accommodate her or not.

There wasn't really a wait, though, before Jacob took the lead, reaching both arms over his head and then abandoning her mouth for only the moment required to yank his shirt off before recapturing her lips in a kiss that had gained a newer, hungrier edge to it.

Ella's arms went around his sleek, muscular torso and her hands got what they'd been aiming for in the first place—the feel of his bare flesh, taut and smooth and hot.

Clearly, pressing skin to skin wasn't something she alone had in mind, because rather than merely cocooning her in his arms once his shirt was out of the way and mouths had met again, Jacob used only one arm to hold her to him and left the other free so he could go to work on the buttons that closed her cardigan up the front.

It wasn't in Ella to complain. Not when complaining was about the last thing on her mind as she felt her nipples harden, eager to have the attention they'd wanted so much more of the night before.

Buttons came free without resistance, and Jacob needed no aid in pushing the top from her shoulders, in discarding it somewhere on the floor behind them and leaving her in her lacy bra.

But even the scant lace over her breasts seemed like armor when his hand cupped one of them and kept her from having all that she craved.

It must not have been enough for him, either, because after a short while of massaging that supersensitive globe over the fabric, he reached around and unhooked the back of her bra, coursing up to her shoulder to finesse the strap down her arm.

His lips left hers again then, and instead he kissed a path along the column of her neck, into the hollow of her throat, trailing the tip of his nose from there to where the bra hardly hugged her now-straining breast and nudging it from her nipple.

Her tightly kerneled nipple that seemed to be demanding his notice all by itself.

Round and round, he circled it with his nose, barely—oh so barely—flicking just the very tip of it with the very tip of his tongue and driving Ella nearly out of her mind before he took it into the dark, warm, wet wonderland of his mouth.

Her spine arched, and a sound rushed out of her that was a cross between a sigh and a moan as the satisfaction of having his mouth on her mingled with the awakening of a whole new spectrum of desires in her.

Desires that began to swirl in the very core of her, gathering power and need with every passing moment, with every drawing of her breast even further into that cavern of pleasure, with every flick and circle of her nipple with his tongue, with every tug of it with tender teeth that teased and tormented and knew just how much she could bear.

Somewhere along the way her bra disappeared, and need made another part of her brain begin to consider how much better everything would be if only there were no clothes between them at all. Especially not those jeans of his, which, while they might fit him to a T, were nothing more than a barrier now.

Sliding her hands from his broad shoulders down the ever-narrowing vee of his back, she hooked her thumbs in his waistband and followed it around to the front where his own burgeoning need for her was not only testing his zipper but was on the verge of bursting above the waistband button.

Ella couldn't help smiling at the proof of how much he wanted her—and how much of him there was *to* want her—any more than she could help popping that button and lowering that zipper to reveal that proof.

The stronger pull of Jacob's mouth on her breast and the deep draw of his breath gave evidence to his own raging needs as she enclosed him in her hand and explored for herself the power and glory that had waited so stoically for her discovery.

But again he was determined not to be alone in any stage of this and as he changed breasts and gave equal time to the one he'd neglected up to then, he made quick work of divesting her of her slacks and bikini panties before writhing out of his jeans, as well, and leaving them both naked.

That was when the true tempest began. When hands knew no hesitation and took possession. When she explored every inch of him and reveled in the feel. When he continued to knead and suckle and torment her yearning breasts even as he reached a hand between her legs and inspired a frenzy of passion, of drive so unimaginable it left Ella breathless.

They were lying on their sides, face-to-face, by then,

and Jacob raised her leg to wrap around his hip, finding that spot between her thighs with more than his hand, more than his talented fingers, easing himself into her inch by incredible inch until he was completely engulfed by the innermost recesses of her body.

He held her against him with one arm around her shoulders while his other arm wrapped her backside and helped her to move with him. To meet him rhythmically, hip to hip. To give way for him to retreat before returning again. And again. Thrusting into her. Deeply, flawlessly into her. Tightening that spiral, that coil that seemed to have originated in the center of her being, that seemed to have been given life by him. Tightening it more and more until it could do nothing but spring free, flinging her into the blinding bliss of a climax so sublime she was only peripherally aware of Jacob reaching his own peak, of his both tensing and plunging so far into her it was as if they had become one entity, one being. One impeccable whole....

And then, completely satiated and spent, muscle by muscle relaxed. Pulses slowed. Breath returned. And Ella dropped her forehead to Jacob's chest.

"Definitely not three feet apart," she whispered.

He flexed within her in response. "Is that where you want me now? Three feet away?" he challenged.

Ella laughed softly. "I don't think so."

"Good, because I'm not going anywhere," he said, holding her all the closer.

He urged her head up with his chin and kissed her again, a long, slow, profoundly intimate kiss before he ended it and said in a raw, ragged, raspy voice, "Not sorry, are you?"

Ella smiled up into that face that was almost too amazing to believe. "Not sorry. You?"

He just smiled back at her, a grin replete enough to be her answer.

Then he closed his eyes as if he couldn't keep them open any longer.

But Ella didn't mind because her own lids were weighty, and there, against Jacob, with Jacob still inside of her, all she wanted to do was sleep, too.

Sleep for just a little while in that single moment when everything seemed made to order and the only force field was the one encircling them both and holding them together.

Chapter Sixteen

After making love a second time—longer, slower and more leisurely than the first—Jacob had carried Champ and led Ella up to his room. He'd laid the sleeping Champ on an armchair rather than putting her in the bed where she usually slept, but he'd pulled the armchair right up to the edge of the mattress so that the puppy didn't wake, go exploring and fall during what was left of the night. Then he and Ella had taken the bed.

Jacob didn't know how long it had been after that that Champ had relocated herself. He only knew that he woke on Sunday morning to Ella lying on her side, facing away from him, him close behind her spooning her body with his, and Champ curled against his nape, her downy head resting on his neck as if it were a chinrest.

He couldn't help smiling at the picture they must

have presented—man, woman and puppy all fitting together like a jigsaw puzzle.

It was nice, though. A nice way to wake up. A much, much nicer way to wake up than waking up alone. In the bed. In the room. In the house. The way he had innumerable times before.

But everything about being there with Ella and Champ was nicer than he could ever remember any time at the house being. Having Ella, in particular, with him, made the place not seem lonely. It made the place actually feel homey. Homey, warm, comfortable, safe.

How strange…

Something must have alerted Champ that he was awake, because the tiny dog raised her head and gave his ear a morning kiss—a signal that the schnauzer wanted to go outside.

In order not to disturb Ella, Jacob slipped his arm from under her pillow, reached up to grab Champ and carefully got out of bed.

Ella stirred, but only slightly, sighing and then settling back into what looked like a peaceful sleep.

For a moment Jacob stood beside the bed, watching her, taking in the sight of her curly, curly hair against the pillow. Of her pale, flawless skin. Of the line of her nose and the soft petal-pink color of her lips. Of one bare shoulder peeking above the edge of the sheet that covered her naked body. And it was as if something inside him had been tapped and a warmth ran all through him.

Stranger still…

Champ began to wiggle, trying to escape Jacob's

hold on her. He set her back on the seat of the armchair, silently moved the chair away from the bed so the puppy couldn't do something mischievous to wake Ella, and then quickly pulled on a pair of sweatpants before catching Champ on the verge of attempting to jump to the floor.

Carrying the ornery pup, Jacob slipped from the room. He went downstairs and through the kitchen, taking the dog out the back door.

There weren't any steps to help Champ down—brick pavers ran from the threshold in a ten-foot square to the edge of the lawn—but he went out with the schnauzer anyway, setting her on the ground. Then he sat on a nearby lawn chair to enjoy the early-morning air.

Maybe he and Ella should have breakfast out here. Maybe he should make eggs and toast, fry some bacon, brew a pot of strong coffee, pour orange juice, and they could have a lazy Sunday morning reading the newspaper on the patio. With Champ frolicking through the grass that was belly-high on her.

That would be very Sunday-morning-at-home-with-the-family, wouldn't it? Jacob mused sardonically.

And even so the appeal of it was astonishingly strong. So strong that it brought his thoughts back to how good it was to have Ella there with him. To how complete she made everything.

Was it possible those old childhood fantasies might not have died after all? That they had been secretly hiding somewhere deep inside him for so many years? Those fantasies of a happy family living here in the house that hadn't seen much happiness or family?

Or was it just that having Ella here had given the old fantasies new life?

Either possibility could be the case, he conceded. But he didn't concede it easily. Because in a world where he didn't get involved in close personal relationships with anyone, where he didn't get attached because no attachments meant no encumbrances and no expectations—and no disappointments—it was tough to admit that someone, anyone, could revitalize something he'd worked to put to rest. Something he wasn't sure he wanted revitalized.

Work—that was what he was about, he reminded himself to balance those other thoughts. Work came first. His job was his life. It was what he could count on. It was what he could count on in a way that he couldn't count on people.

But for no reason he understood, that didn't help now. Thinking about work didn't dissolve the good feelings about Ella and having her there at his house with him. It didn't balance the scales at all.

In fact, it made him think of Gilbert Harrison.

Gilbert Harrison whose job was his whole life. Who was now desperate to save that job because without it he had nothing....

Was that what he wanted for himself? Jacob wondered.

Until that moment it had seemed that it was. Until that moment he wouldn't have had any problem answering an immediate *Yes, that's exactly what I want.*

But now? Now that he'd had even just a brief taste of being in the house with Ella? Of being with her in a variety of venues? Of looking forward to seeing her every night after work? Of doing things with her? Of sharing things with her?

Suddenly he wasn't so sure.

Just work? Nothing but work? For the rest of his days?

Damn, but in the blink of an eye, that had become something that sounded more like a punishment than a life plan.

Jacob glanced around at his yard, wondering if something out there had made him lose touch with reality.

But of course there was nothing that could have accomplished that.

Instead he had to admit that maybe his reality had somehow altered itself in the short while since he'd met Ella.

It was almost as if she'd opened a window he'd closed and boarded up. And there he was, involuntarily looking through that window. At the view beyond it. The view he'd so steadfastly avoided. Or been afraid of.

What was it that Ella had said the night before about his early training teaching him to keep people at a distance to protect himself? Protection. Fear. The two went together hand in hand.

He hadn't ever thought of himself as afraid of anything. Not since he was a kid. He'd been on his own, taken care of himself, dealt head-on with any problem that arose. Certainly that hadn't left him imagining himself *afraid* of anything. But maybe this was a more subtle fear. A more underlying fear. An emotional fear.

He didn't want to admit it. He didn't want to acknowledge it. He sure as hell didn't want it to be true. But now that he really thought about it—without pulling any punches—he knew there was some merit to the theory. He'd devoted himself to work, he'd kept his personal life to an absolute minimum, he'd never let anyone—especially not any woman—get too close. And all because he was so damn afraid that he'd be disappointed by them the way his parents had disappointed him. That he'd be abandoned again.

Hurt again…

"So I let my parents not only wreck my formative years, I let them wreck the rest of my life, too?" he muttered to himself as revelation dawned for him.

Champ trotted over and stood up, bracing her tiny front paws on one of his shins.

Jacob reached down and picked her up, setting her in his lap to stroke her back. "I might have lied to you yesterday, little girl," he confessed to the puppy. "Remember when I was packing and I said I had everything under control when it came to Ella? When it came to my feelings for her? Remember when I said I knew how far to let things go before I cooled it? That what was going on with her was just a temporary situation that I'd end before I was in too deep? Not quite the truth. Any of it."

Champ gave him a forgiving glance and he could have sworn there was a look in her eyes that said he hadn't fooled her for a minute.

So maybe the only one he'd fooled had been himself.

But now that he knew that, now that he was looking through that window Ella had opened, what was going to happen?

Nothing. Not a single thing. Unless he made something happen.

But did he want to make something happen?

If the alternative was ending up like his old college professor, ending up alone with nothing but his job, nothing but working all week and coming to this house to rattle around in on the weekends just the way he'd rattled around in it as a teenager, then he definitely wanted to make something happen. But what *was* that "something" he wanted to make happen?

That didn't require any thought at all.

He knew exactly what he wanted to make happen.

He wanted what he'd had since meeting Ella. What he had with her. He wanted her. Here in his house. With him in the heart of the city. In his life. He wanted them to have their entire futures together.

He wanted to let her in.

Recognizing that, owning up to it, was so monumental for him that for a split second he felt light-headed. Woozy. Off-kilter.

And slightly unsure if he'd gone down the right path with this.

What if he *did* allow her in? What if he lowered his guard and got close to her? What if he started to count on her? On her being there for him? And what if, once he really trusted her, she let him down? The way his parents had?

He knew the answer to all those what-ifs. He knew

because he'd been through it already. Twice. When his father had left and again when his mother had. He knew how he would feel. He knew how lousy it would be. He knew everything he'd go through—the disbelief, the denial, the hope that things would be set right again, the anger and disappointment and disillusionment when things weren't set right again, the depression when he was forced to realize that he was alone—really, really alone.

But even in the midst of reliving the worst times of his life and what he'd gone through, in the midst of reminding himself exactly why he'd built that protective armor around himself and kept himself away from personal relationships, he still saw Ella.

Ella, the way she'd looked when he'd left her in bed a little while ago—soft and cuddly and sexy. But also Ella as the kind of person she was under the surface, too. The kind of person who was unceasingly loyal to her sister, her brother-in-law, her niece. The kind of person who was so tenacious, who had such stick-to-itiveness that she was still doing everything she could to get pregnant even after many failed attempts and discouragements, even without a husband by her side. The kind of person for whom family—the family she had and the family she wanted—were that important. Too important to desert or abandon for any reason.

The kind of person even someone with his issues could trust.

Trust to let into his life.

Jacob held Champ up to look into her eyes. "And that's a damn lucky thing," he said in reference to his own thought about Ella being trustworthy. "Because I don't think life would be worth living from here on without her."

Champ gave her seal of approval by lapping at the tip of his nose and wagging her stubby tail.

"So what do you say we wake Ella up and see if she's willing to give this a shot?"

Jacob took another wet doggy-kiss as agreement.

"That's what I say, too," he said with a laugh.

A laugh and a sudden flood of visions through that window Ella had unblocked.

Visions of this old house blossoming into just that fantasy he'd had of it when he was a boy.

With Ella right there beside him to make it all it could be.

Chapter Seventeen

"Champagne for *breakfast?*" Ella asked in surprise.

"Mimosas—champagne and orange juice," Jacob corrected.

Ella had been awakened an hour earlier by Champ's cold, wet kisses on her cheek. She'd opened her eyes to find Jacob sitting on the edge of the mattress, enjoying the mischief he'd wrought by giving the puppy access to her.

Ella had no complaints, though. She'd laughed and indulged the playful wakeup.

Then, after a few much-warmer, sexier kisses from Jacob that she far preferred to Champ's, Jacob had told her he was serving her breakfast on the patio. He'd suggested that she throw something on and come downstairs.

Since he'd also let her know she had at least forty-five minutes to get there, she'd showered and shampooed her hair, applied a little blush and mascara and slipped into a pair of jeans and a cap-sleeved T-shirt before running a brush and her fingers through her hair to leave it loose.

By the time she'd joined Jacob and Champ, Jacob had laid out a lavish breakfast. Complete with champagne in orange juice.

"This is all so great," she enthused as he held out a chair for her and pushed it into the table once she was seated. "I'm impressed by your culinary abilities and flattered that you would go to so much trouble for me. It feels like we're celebrating."

Jacob did a comical bow at the waist, unwittingly giving Ella a wonderful view of his own jean-clad hips and Henley T-shirted torso.

Then he sat across the glass-topped filigreed patio table and grinned at her. "We *could* be celebrating," he said with a note of mystery and allure in his voice. "Who knows, it just might turn out that we are."

Ella laughed. "It's Sunday morning—I believe there's a law against being cryptic on Sunday morning. Especially before breakfast."

"You want it straight up, huh?"

There was far, far too much innuendo in that question not to make her laugh again. And tingle all over with the memories the innuendo inspired of the previous night they'd spent together. With the thought that maybe they could do it again before leaving here today....

"I like things straight up," she answered coyly, unable to suppress an insinuative smile of her own.

"I brought Champ out a while ago and did some thinking. Some realizing, actually," Jacob informed her then.

There was just enough of an alteration in his voice to alert Ella to the fact that they were suddenly not merely exchanging sexual banter that might lead them back to the bedroom. Beneath that cat-that-ate-the-canary teasing, he was serious.

"Thinking and realizing…" Ella repeated, adjusting her own attitude. "What about?"

"You. This place. You and me. In this place."

Which told her nothing, so her only answer was to urge him to go on.

"I was thinking about what a difference you've made for me just since we met. About how much you bring to my life. I was thinking that maybe that old childhood fantasy of having a family of my own, here in this house, is still alive and well after all. That the thought of you and me as a family is a pretty good one."

Ella was certain that her shock showed in her expression. "That's a lot of thinking," she said, working to sort through it. And trying to figure out what he might mean and where he might be headed. Trying, too, to contain the little thrills his words were sending all through her so she didn't get ahead of herself.

"That was only the starting point," Jacob said with that half smile he sometimes flashed that made her pulse quicken. Then he continued to lay out all that had gone through his mind while she'd been sleeping upstairs.

"What it boils down to," he finally concluded, "is that even though we haven't known each other a long time, we've clicked. We've connected in a way some people never do. We've found something—something pretty incredible—in each other, in being together. And I want it to go on." His dark blue eyes held hers and his voice grew intimate again. "I want it to go on and on and on…"

She definitely wasn't inclined to put an end to what had begun between them, she knew that. Even if her head *was* spinning so much she found it difficult to grasp most of what he was saying. "It has been amazing," she concurred.

"You're not eating your breakfast," he said, despite the fact that he hadn't touched his food, either.

"You're giving me a lot to digest without it," Ella joked. Then, hoping for a little more clarity, she said, "So you want to celebrate that we met?"

He shook his head. "I'm hoping we can celebrate more than that. I'm hoping we can celebrate where we're going from here."

"And where would you like that to be?"

"Everywhere. I want you in my life forever. I want us to have, to build, a whole life together."

Ella was conscious of the fact that her eyes had widened at that. Widened enough that the reaction made Jacob laugh yet again. "I know," he said in response to her expression. "Fast—this has been really fast—and I'm dumping a ton on you all at once. It must sound like I want us to do something crazy when that's not what I'm saying. In fact, in one way, I want us to slow something down—"

"Good," Ella said as if she were relieved to hear

that, when she continued to be unclear about what exactly he did want.

"Let's put the infertility stuff on hold," he said then. "I want us to concentrate on each other. I want to concentrate on getting to know everything there is to know about you. I want you to concentrate on getting to know everything there is to know about me. I want every minute I can have with you—alone with you—for a while so we can focus on just us. Once we've done that, I want us to move on to the next step—to sealing our future together, to formally making a life together, a home. Then I promise you I will leave no stone unturned in getting you pregnant."

He finished that with another of those sexy smiles and enough innuendo to let her know he was referring to the making-love part of that equation as well as the medical portion.

But this time his words had a less positive effect on her. Because this time what he was saying struck a nerve.

"I can't put off the infertility stuff, or trying to get pregnant, any more than I already have."

"It won't be for long," he promised. "Look how far we've come in such a short while. I just want some time with you first. Alone. Without pregnancy hormones ruling things, without needing to be thinking about a pregnancy or a coming baby. Is that so much to ask? Especially when you'll have your own personal infertility specialist at your disposal once we're both ready?"

Ella understood his perspective. She knew that after the neglected childhood he'd had he must surely crave some personal, one-on-one attention from someone he cared about before introducing a child into the mix to pull that attention off him. And he deserved that. He had it coming. It was something she would have liked to be able to give him.

But she couldn't do what she'd done before with Brandon. She couldn't allow the deep need she had for a child to be put off again. Not by anyone. Time was against her, and the older she got—even if it was only another year—the more likely it was that she would never be able to conceive. Regardless of how good he was at what he did for a living or how much of his expertise she had at her disposal.

Besides, even though he wasn't completely disregarding her needs, her goals, her most desperate desire, he wasn't putting them first, either. And she was very, very afraid of heading down any path where what she wanted, what she needed, came second again.

"I can't do it," she said.

"You can't do what?"

"I can't put off the infertility stuff. Not for any amount of time."

His smile turned a bit sly. "I'm your doctor and I say you can."

"You *aren't* actually my doctor yet and, doctor or not, you can't give me any guarantees that one minute of putting off trying to get pregnant won't be one minute too long," she said, feeling a hint of anger beginning to know that Jacob—of all people—would diminish in any way the importance of time in this situation.

"Nobody can give guarantees, no—"

"You didn't even think I had much of a chance going into the alternative medicine study," she cut him off to remind him. "You and I both know that whatever chance I do have isn't going to get better by wasting what little time I may have."

"But if it doesn't happen we'll take an alternate route. There's surrogacy. There's adoption—"

And those were options she *would* take if she had to. But if she stopped trying now and then didn't get pregnant and had to take one of those other options, she'd always wonder if she might have been able to carry and have her own child if she just hadn't let yet another man postpone things for her. Another man who seemed to be overlooking just how important this was to her.

She shook her head, her anger growing. "If there's any way I can get pregnant, that's what I want."

Jacob's face sobered, hardened, and she saw the return of the man she'd met the first day in his office as even his posture changed and he sat up taller in his chair, drew his shoulders back and became an imposing figure once again. "Or maybe what you *don't* want is me."

"It isn't that. Not at all," she said in a hurry, discovering just how much truth was in her words as they came out, but still feeling rumblings of rage at his position on the subject. "This time with you has been as incredible for me as it has for you. The end of every time with you has seemed to come too fast and all I can think about is how long it will be before I can see you again. Everything you've said this morning has given me goose bumps that tell me just how glad I am to hear it—everything except putting my attempts to conceive on hold. And that I can't—I *won't*—do. Either you want kids as much as I do and right away or you don't," she finished, a note of challenge, of ultimatum in her voice.

"And if I just want them slightly down the road instead of instantly?" he said, matching her tone.

Ella shook her head. "I can't wait."

"We need some time alone," he insisted. "We need to learn each other's rhythms, quirks. We need to learn how to read each other. We have to know where our strengths and weaknesses lie as a couple. We need to know how to help each other and nurture each other before we can do that for a baby. We need to be a team, a consolidated unit, a united front, before we're parents."

Of course those were good and valid points. Of course people should have that wealth of knowledge and insight about each other and be that kind of couple before they had a child. Ideally. But the ideal couldn't always be met. It certainly hadn't been for him and he'd still managed to grow up to be a successful adult, which was what Ella told him.

"And I can't wait for everything to be perfect beforehand," she repeated more forcefully. "I don't have that luxury."

"So neither do I, is that it?" he challenged, sounding once again as brusque as he had before she'd gotten to see his softer side.

Ella raised her chin. "You can have anything you want," she said defensively.

"Except you."

"Except me not trying to get pregnant right away."

He raised both hands in frustration. "Can't you see how that would make our start different? More complicated? That we—that any couple—needs time alone first?"

"I can see all that," Ella admitted. "I just can't do it. I can't risk losing what could be my last window of opportunity."

"I will make sure you have babies," he swore, his voice rising enough to alarm Champ who awoke from her nap in a patch of sunshine on the grass.

"You may be able to make sure I have them *someday,* that someone else will carry and give birth to them if I can't when that day comes. But then I'll be left wondering if I could have had the experience—that experience I want more than you can know—if only I hadn't let you delay it for me the way Brandon did. And that isn't something I want between us."

Champ came to the side of Jacob's chair, and he picked her up, holding her against his middle in a way that made Ella feel as if he were putting the puppy between them to shield himself from her.

"I can't believe you won't just let it ride for a little while," he said angrily.

"I can't believe you can't understand what this means to me," she countered, maintaining her stance through a force of will when it was so tempting to relinquish it, to trust that the great Dr. Jacob Weber would be able to work a miracle to get her pregnant if only she gave him some concentrated time and attention first.

When it was so tempting to give in to what he was asking of her in order to have him....

But she couldn't. Not already knowing the regret of sacrificing her own strongest desires for someone else once before and losing both him and the babies she might have had if she just hadn't waited.

Neither of them said anything for a long time.

And then, when Ella could bear the silence no more, she stood.

"I'm sorry."

Jacob just looked down at Champ, petting the puppy gently and not acknowledging Ella or her apology.

"I'll call my sister," she said. "Sara will drive out and pick me up so you don't have to take me back into town."

Still no response.

And while Ella was tempted to beg Jacob not to leave things like that, not to be so stubborn, not to erect those walls around himself, she knew the only thing that was going to break down this wall was for her to concede what she held closest to her own heart.

And she just couldn't do it.

Chapter Eighteen

The three weeks that brought Ella to the end of September were the longest of her life. She didn't see Jacob again, once she'd left him on the patio of his family home near Saunders University. Neither he nor Champ had been anywhere in sight when she'd come downstairs with her bag packed to wait for her sister to pick her up, and even though she hadn't been kicked out of the alternative medicine study, her path never crossed Jacob's during any of the four nights per week she saw Dr. Schwartz in Jacob's office.

The sole contact she had from him came through his nurse, who informed her that Dr. Weber would not be performing the in vitro procedures that were to follow Dr. Schwartz's treatment. Dr. Weber, the nurse said, had contacted Ella's previous specialist and convinced him to take over from there.

Ella was grateful that Jacob wasn't being vindictive. That he hadn't thrown her out of the study or left her in the lurch for the in vitro to follow. Grateful that he hadn't at all sabotaged this last chance she felt she had to conceive a child.

But she still felt awful.

She missed Jacob horribly. She thought about him all the time. She had trouble concentrating on even her biggest cases at work. And knowing, or even assuming, that when she was in Jacob's office, he was close by made her ache with wanting to see him. To talk to him. To hear his voice. To have him put his arms around her and tell her he'd changed his mind.

But that never happened, and Ella didn't waver from her own position, either. She just couldn't do what she'd done before in letting a man postpone what she wanted until it was too late for her. She just couldn't.

So when Dr. Schwartz released her at the end of the month and asked only that Ella contact her in three months to report any success or failure of the ensuing in vitro procedures, Ella could do nothing but cast a glance in the direction of the firmly closed door to Jacob's inner office and walk out.

"Date of your last period?"

It was a question Ella had answered more times than she could count, and yet now, as she sat alone in an examining room, it repeated itself in her mind with a whole new impact.

The date of her last period…

That's what the nurse had asked her several minutes before.

Ella had taken her day planner from her purse and checked it before she was able to answer the nurse who was doing the routine inquiry for her gynecologist.

"That's longer than it should be," the nurse had responded to the date Ella had given her. "Is it possible you could already be pregnant?"

Ella had laughed. "Pregnant? That's why I'm here— to *get* pregnant."

But then she'd thought about it. Thought about that night she'd spent with Jacob at his house three weeks before. About the fact that they hadn't bothered with protection.

And even though it didn't seem possible, she'd had to amend her answer to the nurse.

"I guess I *could* be," she'd said. "But it's highly unlikely…"

"Unlikely or not, let's do a urine test, see what that tells us," the nurse suggested. "It can't do any harm."

So Ella had given the specimen required and was now waiting in the exam room for the results.

And telling herself it couldn't possibly be…

Then the exam room door opened again after a perfunctory tap from outside.

Only, rather than the nurse returning as Ella had expected, she was surprised to see her doctor.

With a bemused expression on his face.

"Lionel?" she said.

A smile diffused some of the doctor's bemusement.

"I don't know what you did in the last month—well, I guess I know what you must have done—but the test we've just run on your sample is positive. For pregnancy. You're pregnant, Ella."

If it was possible for the earth to stand still, it seemed to Ella as if that was what happened at that moment.

Then her doctor added, "You're finally going to be a mom."

And Jacob was going to be a dad....

Her doctor reached a hand to her arm. "Are you feeling okay? The color just drained out of your face right before my eyes."

"I'm okay," Ella managed. Then, sounding as shocked as she felt, she whispered, "Are you sure?"

The doctor laughed. "We'll do a blood test to *make* sure, and I'll put a rush on it to get the results by tomorrow because I know how much this means to you. But these quickie tests we do now are pretty accurate. I wouldn't get your hopes up otherwise. I'm reasonably sure that you're going to have a baby."

Ella's appointment with her gynecologist was at the very end of the day so she went straight home afterward.

As she arrived at her apartment, unlocked her door and went inside, it occurred to her that she had no concrete memory of the drive. Her mind was too busy reliving what had just taken place.

Pregnant...

She closed the door behind herself, dropped her purse and keys on the table and went to sit on her couch, staring ahead at nothing, just thinking over and over again, *I'm pregnant....*

There was a part of her that had come to believe she might never hear that said of her, and that part was in deep disbelief.

Pregnant...

A baby...

I'm going to have a baby....

And then she started to cry.

The tears were tears of joy. Of having been given a gift she'd been terrified she might never receive. Of the pure miracle that it had come to be. That she—Ella Gardner—after too many medical procedures and so much worrying and work and heartache and disappointment and emotional and physical pain, was going to have a baby of her own. It had finally happened.

"A baby," she said out loud in her apartment, the first time she'd uttered the word since being informed that she was pregnant. It made her laugh. A little hysterically, but there she was, laughing and crying and thinking that it didn't seem real. Or possible. Or true.

"But it *is* true," she said to herself as if to convince a naysayer. "For no reason I can begin to understand, one night with Jacob did what nothing and no one before him could."

And she wanted to tell him.

That struck her out of the blue.

It also struck her hard enough to dry her tears and sober her laughter.

In amazement she realized that her first inclination wasn't to call her sister or any of her friends—people she was, and had been, genuinely close to for her whole life, people who had been through all the infertility trials and tribulations with her, people who would love to know. But no, her first inclination wasn't to call any of those people. It was to tell Jacob.

As if telling him—and him alone—would make it real. Would make it true.

As if it wouldn't be real or true until she *did* tell him.

But he certainly wasn't someone she could just pick up the phone and call. Not now. Not the way things had been left between them. Not after the cold war of the past three weeks.

And would he even want to know? she wondered.

He didn't want to see her. He didn't want to talk to her. He hadn't wanted to have a baby with her until some indefinite time in the future.

So maybe he wouldn't want to know.

Having a baby was so important to her that it was difficult for her to fathom that the father of that baby wouldn't want to know about it. Wouldn't embrace the idea now that it had happened. Wouldn't be thrilled.

But this was Jacob, she reminded herself. Jacob, who was not the most easygoing guy in the world. Jacob, whose own parents had deserted him, had left him to fend for himself as an adolescent. Jacob, who had—for what seemed to have been the first time—let down the facade of arrogance that had protected him and allowed someone to get close to him only to have that someone reject him.

That someone who was Ella.

Ella who was now pregnant with Jacob's baby.

She rolled her eyes heavenward and said to the Fates, "You just couldn't make it easy, could you?"

Jacob Weber as the father of her baby...

She *could* not tell him, she thought, sinking back into the cushions of the couch, collapsing a little beneath the weight of all that was going through her mind.

Even if she notified Dr. Schwartz that she'd gotten pregnant, no one need ever know that it hadn't been from in vitro procedures following the alternative treatments. No one would suspect it had happened any other way. Probably not even Jacob. And she'd still have her baby. Without any other attachments or complications or ties. Her baby and hers alone. Free and clear. Without any interference.

Without Jacob.

But that image just wasn't as satisfying as the image of having his baby with him. Of having him share in all of it.

Or was Jacob not the only one for whom fantasies could reawaken? Was she having a resurgence of her old fantasy? The one she'd hoped would become real— a traditional family, complete with a mother and father? The one that, when the divorce had happened, she'd had to accept could well remain only a fantasy.

Was the inclination to fulfill that traditional image making a comeback for her now? And was it giving her some kind of illusion that things with Jacob could work out if only she told him about the baby? An illusion in which he cast aside all of his own desires not to have a child right away and was simply thrilled that this was how things had ended up?

Somehow that didn't sound like Jacob. Jacob who was too proud and who had a streak of stubbornness so strong that he'd suffered hardship, loneliness and poverty rather than let anyone in the world know his parents had squandered their money and left him to fend for himself.

So maybe it was better not to tell him. Not to even hope to have him participate, Ella told herself then. Besides, even if she told him and his reaction wasn't altogether negative, what kind of father would he be? What if, as a parent, he was the surly, contrary, hard-to-get-close-to Jacob? Because if that were the case, that wouldn't make him a great father. Or a person she would want to parent a child with. It wouldn't make for a happy home. Not for any of them.

Yet even as Ella considered that, she couldn't quite believe that would happen. Not when she recalled his tender, loving, patient care of Champ; his gentle nurturing of the tiny puppy; the fact that he had not only rescued the schnauzer, but hand-fed her, pampered her, devoted himself to her, to keep her alive. Not when he still carried her around in his pocket and picked restaurants that could be persuaded to let him bring her in rather than leave her alone for too long.

And there had been Janey, too, Ella remembered now. Jacob had indulged her niece the night he'd met Janey at her third birthday party. That had definitely come from Jacob's softer core, not from the gruff outer persona.

The softer core that had shown itself more and more with Ella. That she knew was there in abundance.

No, Jacob might be a wonderful dad. If only he wanted to be.

But that was still the question, wasn't it? Did he *want* to be? Or, at least, did he want to be a father ahead of the schedule he'd set out for them?

Those were questions she couldn't answer. Questions only Jacob could answer.

And he could only answer them if she let him know there was going to be a baby.

Was she rationalizing? she asked herself. Was she using this turn of events as a way to get back in with Jacob?

And what if he did let her back in only because of this—only out of feelings of obligation and duty and responsibility—and not because he wanted her or the baby?

That wouldn't be good.

Not for her. Not for the baby. Not for him.

So maybe she shouldn't tell him, she thought, vacillating yet again.

Maybe she should just work at forgetting him. At putting him out of her mind. At going on with her life without him and counting herself lucky that they'd even met, that fate had put them together for that brief time so she could finally conceive, Maybe that was all that was meant for them.

Ella honestly didn't know which course she should take.

But ultimately, once she'd gone through just about all of it in her head again, the conclusion she came to was that the course in which she simply accepted that fate had put them together only briefly to make a baby and that she shouldn't even tell Jacob she was pregnant wasn't the course she *wanted* to take.

Not when it really, truly meant the end of things between herself and Jacob. When it meant seeing him in his child but not having him in her life. When it meant that she hadn't at least *tried* to sort through this with him and possibly reach that happily-ever-after ending.

And if he *didn't* want her or the baby?

Well, at least she'd still have her baby.

It was just that, now that there *was* going to be a baby—a baby of Jacob's—it would be nice to have Jacob, too.

More than nice.

And she realized she wanted him every bit as much as she had ever wanted a child.

Chapter Nineteen

The next day was Friday, and since Ella didn't have to be in court, she took a personal day. She didn't accomplish anything staying at home and pacing, but she knew she wouldn't have been able to get a single iota of work done at the office. At least in her apartment she didn't have to pretend not to be completely and utterly distracted.

Her gynecologist didn't call with the results of the blood test until nearly five o'clock, and once she hung up the phone she sat on her sofa to absorb the final confirmation.

She was, indeed, pregnant.

And that meant that she was going to do what she'd spent the past twenty-four hours fretting about.

She was going to see Jacob.

"But you're not going to get there from this couch," she told herself.

She also wasn't going to face him for the first time in three weeks without putting some effort into her appearance, either, so she took a deep breath and got to her feet.

She showered with the expensive gel she saved for special occasions, shampooed and conditioned her hair, shaved her legs, moisturized, perfumed and generally did every girly thing she could think to do to make herself appealing.

Then she donned a pair of black slacks that she knew made her rear end look better than any other pants she owned, and added a sexy, mesh off-the-shoulder blouse that showed the form-fitting, bra-strap camisole beneath it.

She put extra care into her makeup, even dusting her eyelids with pale taupe shadow and applying a barely there lipstick that had promised to be kissable.

She left her hair loose, finger-combing it to what she hoped was a sexy cascade of come-hither curls, and then she slipped her feet into a pair of two-inch, high-heeled mules she'd paid half a week's salary for.

"If this doesn't knock him dead nothing will," she told her reflection in the mirror.

Then she headed out of her apartment before she lost her courage.

The trouble was by the time she'd driven to Jacob's town house, her courage had wilted anyway.

Still, she didn't merely drive by, the way she was tempted to. She forced herself to park in the spot on the street two doors down from his, where she sat staring ahead at his place.

Listening to the sound of her own heartbeat racing so fast she could feel it.

There was a light on in the living room window of Jacob's place—it seemed he was spending Friday night at home. But since the drapes were pulled she had no indication of whether or not he was alone. For all she knew, he could have a date in there with him. Someone he'd known before their short-lived time together or someone he'd met in the past three weeks.

That possibility didn't help her nerves any.

But she'd decided that this was what she was going to do, so she wouldn't let herself chicken out.

Still, the walk from her car to the town house felt like miles, and with every step she wondered if she was doing the right thing.

Then she rang the doorbell and, the moment she'd done it, was struck by the awkwardness of showing up like this, unannounced, dressed to the nines, to tell a man who didn't want to see her that he'd gotten her pregnant.

But before she could turn tail and run, or hide in the bushes—the way she was fleetingly inclined to do—the door opened.

And there was Jacob.

Ella's brain suddenly fired in too many directions to hit anything, and she just stood there for a moment, dumbstruck and staring at the big, tall, staggeringly handsome man dressed in jeans and a plain red crewneck T-shirt, holding Champ under one arm—probably so she couldn't run out the door when he opened it.

Unfortunately the expression on Jacob's face was not one of warmth and welcome and pleasure to see her. His brows pulled together over the bridge of his nose and those dark, dark-blue eyes of his pierced right through her.

"Ella?" he said, clearly to prompt her to speak.

"Hi," she responded, knowing it was lame, hating that that was the best she could come up with and wishing her greeting had at least been more than a bare whisper that announced just how unsure she was of herself.

She tried for more power and added, "I'd like to talk to you."

Jacob merely went on pinning her to that spot with his gaze, frowning with an intensity that made her want to run the other way.

But she didn't. She reminded herself that she'd faced him down once before—that first day she'd met him—and she'd ended up getting what she wanted. Ultimately *exactly* what she'd wanted, even if not in the manner she'd anticipated. But still, recalling that initial meeting gave her the impetus to stay where she was.

"I have to tell you something," she said then, calling on her courtroom voice to project more confidence than she felt.

Jacob stepped aside then, allowing her in without invitation.

Champ, at least, was happy to see her. When Jacob set the puppy down she ran to where Ella had ended up—standing in the center of the living room. Champ stood on her hind legs, bracing her front paws on Ella's shin, and Ella bent over and picked her up, grateful for the warm, furry little dog as moral support.

Jacob didn't quite join them in the living room. He made it as far as the archway that connected it to the entry, leaning one broad shoulder against the side edge and crossing his arms over his massive chest as he resettled his gaze on Ella and returned to simply watching her and waiting.

This wasn't going well, and Ella knew it. What she was the most worried about was that it was going so badly because Jacob didn't want anything more to do with her. And if that was the case, then she decided she should find it out before she went all the way to telling him about the pregnancy.

"I'm sorry if I've come at a bad time," she began.

"I just got home from the office—that doesn't make it a good time or a bad one," he said with a full measure of his well-known arrogance in his tone.

"Maybe I shouldn't have bothered you," she said, thinking out loud more than fishing for any kind of reassurance.

"I'm not bothered," he said.

Even though his attitude remained the same, Ella caught his gaze wavering. Enough so that she knew he was taking in her appearance at least, and at best maybe liking what he saw or liking the fact that he was getting to see it again.

Whatever was going through his mind, the fact that there was some indication that his reception might not be completely negative gave her a modicum of encouragement.

"Will you stop?" she said then.

One eyebrow arched. "Will I stop what?"

"Being *that* Jacob," she answered.

"Being *what* Jacob?"

"The one you were when you didn't want anyone knowing what was going on in your home life. The one who makes sure you keep people at a distance. The one we moved past. Be the other Jacob—the one you were the last time we were together."

"You didn't want that one, either, as I recall."

She'd hurt him. She could see it suddenly, lurking behind his eyes, in the defensiveness—the protectiveness—in those arms crossed over his chest, in the stance that kept him far away from her.

"I did want that one," she said softly, thinking that if she didn't go out on a limb *he* never would. "I still want that one."

The single eyebrow went up again. "Is that what you came to tell me?"

A tiny note of hope echoed in his voice and it broke Ella's heart.

"That and more," she said. "I'm just not sure you're going to like the *more* part of it."

Champ wiggled in her arms, alerting Ella to the fact that she was holding the puppy too tight. Rather than risk hurting her, Ella set her on the floor.

As if the schnauzer could sense the tension in the room and wanted to hide from it, Champ ran into the dining room and ducked into her crate there.

"What's going on, Ella?" Jacob demanded, cutting to the chase.

Ella took a deep breath, sighed it out and decided to take the plunge. "I'm pregnant," she said in such a soft voice she wasn't sure he had even heard it until she saw what her doctor had apparently seen in her the day before—she saw the color drain from Jacob's face.

"Pregnant," he repeated dubiously. "The study just ended. At best you've only had time to get into your doctor for a first visit."

"Yesterday," Ella confirmed. "That was when the nurse realized what I overlooked because I've been too engrossed in thinking about you for the past three weeks. I'd missed a cycle. They did the test in the office. It was positive, but to make sure they took blood and called me today."

"And you're pregnant?"

She nodded.

And then waited.

She could tell that shock was Jacob's strongest reaction. And that he needed to let what she'd told him sink in. But she was on pins and needles while she let that happen.

"Pregnant?" he repeated yet again a few moments later, his tone no longer abrasive or harsh, stripped down to that Jacob she'd been longing to have returned to her.

"Barely, but yes," she said.

"My house," he said, piecing things together.

Ella nodded a second time.

Another moment of silence fell, and she couldn't help wondering if he was still trying to process this or if he was thinking of how to congratulate her and send her on her way.

Then he let out a chuckle and said, "Well, this certainly feels better than any of the other times I've gotten women pregnant."

She couldn't help cracking a smile at that.

"So what now?" he asked.

She wasn't sure what that meant, either.

"I know what I'd like to happen now," she ventured. "But this—a baby—isn't what you wanted, so I guess it's up to you."

"It isn't that I didn't want a baby," he amended. "I just wanted a little while alone with you before."

"Couldn't eight and a half months be enough?" she asked quietly.

He didn't even attempt to camouflage the look that went from the top of her head to the tips of her toes and back again this time. Only now he also didn't hide his appreciation of it.

"To tell you the truth I've been doing a lot of thinking about us and our situation in the past three weeks, and today I put in a call to Kim Schwartz to ask her what she thought about continuing to treat you with Chinese medicine the way she has been for another two or three months."

"Why?" Ella asked, confused.

"Because I was thinking that maybe you and I could come to a minor compromise. That maybe if Kim would go on treating you with the course that was meant to heighten your fertility and chances for conception, then she could keep that at an optimal level while we had a few months of at-home honeymoon. I was thinking that maybe then—if you knew we weren't wasting *too* much of your window of opportunity and were adding more of the treatment intended to increase the chance of pregnancy, we could still have what I proposed that morning at the house."

Jacob paused and pushed off the edge of the wall, coming to stand nearer to her before he continued.

"But even if that didn't work out, I was going to just give in," he confessed. "Because the way I felt as a kid when my parents bailed was nothing compared to the way I've felt since you left that morning. So eight and a half months alone with you is still better than nothing. Much, much better than nothing."

"Then why were you so mean when you opened the door and saw me standing there?" Ella demanded.

Jacob smiled a crooked smile and let his eyes roll slowly down her body once more. "Looking like that? I was afraid you were on your way to a hot date and had just stopped by to return something of mine that might have gotten mixed in with your things."

That made Ella smile, too. "I just wanted to be irresistible."

"You succeeded," he said, taking her into his arms and kissing her with a hunger that let her know he had missed her as much as she'd missed him.

A hunger that flared instantly to prolong that kiss, to add more to it until mouths were opened wide and tongues were reacquainting themselves and Ella's arms were around Jacob, too, her hands splayed against his broad back.

"We need to talk," she said breathlessly after several moments.

"We will," he promised, recapturing her mouth with his a split second later and pulling her even closer against him.

It occurred to Ella that perhaps she should insist that they do the rest of the talking first. But by then his hands had begun to slip her clothes off, and her body was alive with the needs only he could arouse and satisfy, and talking suddenly seemed less important than meeting those needs.

She yanked his T-shirt free of his jeans and nearly ripped it off him, casting it aside to join her own tops on the floor somewhere out of the way.

She cooperated when he divested her of her slacks, too, and wasted precious little time opening the button and zipper of his jeans and pushing them down far enough for him to rid himself of them completely.

And then there they were again, on another couch, as hands explored and so did mouths. As fingers titillated and teased and turned on. As tongues sought and found secret places and brought them both to new heights of desire. As bodies came together, fitting perfectly, moving rhythmically, each aiding the other in reaching a climax so powerful that if Ella had returned from it and found the entire room disrupted, she wouldn't have been surprised.

When it was over and they were both breathing normally again, Jacob rolled them to lie on their sides and pressed a tender kiss to the top of her head.

"I love you," he said then, sincerely. "Have I told you that?"

"You know you haven't," Ella said with a laugh. "It's nice to hear, though." She angled her head backward to look into his face. "But would you love me more if you weren't getting a package deal?"

He smiled broadly and shook his head. "I couldn't love you more. And for the record, I never said I didn't want a baby at all, I just wanted to wait a little while so I could have you to myself."

"I'll make sure the pregnancy doesn't invade everything," she assured him.

"And miss out on a minute of it? I don't think so. Just don't forget I'm around in the process."

That made her laugh and flex her hips up into his where they still met at the joining of their bodies. "You're pretty unforgettable. Besides, I'm so in love with you you're not likely to slip my mind."

That made him smile and look satisfied and smug at the same time.

He bent his head enough to kiss her on the mouth again and then looked down into her eyes. "A baby, huh?"

"A baby," Ella confirmed with a voice full of joy that could finally be completely unfurled.

"I did what no one else could," he said with a proud grin.

"And you're feeling very cocky about it," Ella accused.

"It *is* something," he insisted.

"Yes, it is," Ella agreed, kissing his chest and resting her forehead there afterward as she felt him relaxing all around her, inside of her.

Ella relaxed, too, then. Feeling happier than she ever remembered feeling.

And as Jacob's breathing grew deeper and steadier, she couldn't help thinking that maybe destiny's hand had been at work in her life all along, keeping her from getting pregnant no matter what she did, until the one man who was meant for her came along to do the job.

Until Jacob came along.

Thinking, too, that if that was the case, every ounce of the heartache and disappointment and frustration she'd ever suffered had been worth it.

Everything she'd ever gone through had been worth it, if it had all led her to him.

To him and to finally having a baby. *His* baby. The baby she'd always dreamed of.

And if a few warm tears rolled out of the corner of her eye and onto Jacob's chest? She knew he wouldn't mind. Because they were only tears of the purest kind.

They were tears of utter and complete joy.

* * * * *

Look for the next book in the new
Special Edition continuity, MOST LIKELY TO...
Coming in November 2005
Secrets of a Good Girl by Jen Safrey
Eric Barnes has agreed to go to London and
find Cassidy Maxwell, the former student who
may hold the key to the defense of beloved
Professor Harrison. But when Eric finds Cassidy,
he uncovers a well of secrets—
and the love of a lifetime!
Available wherever Silhouette Books are sold.

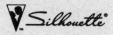

SILHOUETTE

SPECIAL EDITION™

presents

the first book in a heartwarming new series by

Kristin Hardy

Because there's
no place like home
for the holidays...

WHERE THERE'S SMOKE

(November 2005, SE#1720)

Sloane Hillyard took a very personal interest in her work inventing fire safety equipment—after all, her firefighter brother had died in the line of duty. And when Boston fire captain Nick Trask signed up to test her inventions, things got even more personal... their mutual attraction set off alarms. But could Sloane trust her heart to a man who risked his life and limb day in and day out?

Available November 2005 at your favorite retail outlet.

Where love comes alive™

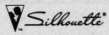

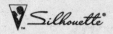

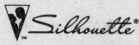

COMING NEXT MONTH

SPECIAL EDITION